MARY BILLITER

RULE
BREAKERS

For information, contact the publisher, Hot Tree Publishing.

WWW.HOTTREEPUBLISHING.COM

EDITING: HOT TREE EDITING

COVER DESIGNER: CLAIRE SMITH

FORMATTING: RMGRAPHX

ARTWORK: JCH STUDIOS

ISBN-10: 1-925655-13-X

ISBN-13: 978-1-925655-13-1

10 9 8 7 6 5 4 3 2 1

Life is short, break the rules,

Forgive quickly,

Kiss SLOWLY.

Love truly.

Laugh uncontrollably

And never regret

ANYTHING

That makes you smile

-Mark Twain

ALSO BY MARY **BILLITER**

RESORT **ROMANCES**

Do Not Disturb : Book 1
Escape Clause : Book 2
Rule Breakers: Book 3
Spirited Away : Book 4

RESORT
ROMANCES
BY MARY BILLITER
Opening Soon
The Historic Wyoming
Point Resort
Cheyenne WY
"Do Not Disturb"
Huntington Beach, CA
"ESCAPE CLAUSE"
The Point Resort
Newport OR
CANADA
MEXICO
"Rule Breakers"
YOUR NEXT BOOK
DESTINATION:
the Waterfront Point
HUNTINGTON BEACH, CA

CHAPTER **ONE**

"Welcome to the Waterfront Point Resort."

The brim of her baseball cap shielded her face, but when I stepped out of my car and there were no longer shadows blocking my view, I saw that her blue eyes were an exotic contrast against her butterscotch-kissed skin and silky black hair.

"Good evening, sir. I'm Carmen, and I will be taking care of your car."

Good evening, indeed.

"Hello, Carmen." I extended my hand. "I'm Hunter, and I'll be your guest for the evening." I cleared my throat. "I mean, my car, *my car* will be your guest or...." I curtly shook my head, but the damage was done. *I'm an idiot.* "The keys are inside."

When she smiled, her full lips looked like a luscious raspberry that turned my stomach inside out. *Damn, the girl's fine.*

The setting sun caught the vintage Point Resort logo

stitched in gold on the bill of her cap. It glistened as brightly as her skin. My cell phone vibrated fin the pocket of my dinner jacket to remind me that I was already late for my meeting with the founder and owner of the hotel, but I didn't care. *Michael Harpington can wait.*

"So, Hunter…" Her voice was as smooth as the hair that hung from the back of her cap and swayed in a steady beat like a metronome. Every time she moved, her hair swung with a mesmerizing cadence. "…are you here on business or pleasure?"

"My business is pleasure," I said, inches from her. I knew I was crowding her personal space, hell, I was in her bubble, but I didn't care. This woman smelled like coconuts and suntan lotion, and she radiated warmth. She was everything that made the Southern California beach, which roared in the distance, irresistible. I wanted to soak her in as long as I could. "Why do you ask?" I raised an eyebrow.

She cocked the tip of her cap toward the back of my car. "Just wondered if you had any bags to check in."

Oh. I felt like an ass, and I'm sure it showed on my face. The downside to being a pale Irishman was that when I was embarrassed, it revealed itself like a freshly boiled lobster, only nowhere near as enticing or desired.

"Bags, right. I've got one." I nodded toward the rear of my rented silver Mercedes. "But I can get it—unless that's breaking the rules."

"I'm kind of a rule breaker," she said, and then arched an eyebrow at me with a smile.

I laughed. "Good to know." *Is she flirting with me?*

Before I could find out, a hotel guest walked up the drive. Carmen's face flushed. "Getting your bag is no trouble." She politely looked up at me. "If I may?"

"Right." I stepped aside and she reached into the car for the key fob, which she pointed toward the trunk. "Anything for a fellow rule breaker."

She said nothing, nor did she look again in my direction. I could have been covered in chocolate syrup and had hundred-dollar bills stuck all over me, and she still wouldn't have been interested in me. A modern version of being tarred and feathered, and it wouldn't even make her look twice in my direction. *Epic fail.*

Hopefully my dinner with Michael would go more smoothly.

CHAPTER **TWO**

"Who's the hottie with a body?"

"You're working late." I glanced at my watch, hoping to divert the conversation. "It's well past five and quitting time. Heck, it's almost seven."

"Yeah, I've got a marketing program to develop and no new ideas. And Bogart's working the overnight so there's no rush to get home to an empty house. So, seriously, what's his name?" She stood beside me, not as close as Hunter had, but she wasn't going to leave until I answered.

"Who?" It was a long shot, but maybe Katie suffered from short-term memory loss like Dory, the fish from my nephew's favorite movie.

"Good try." She elbowed me. "The guy that just left. Who is he?"

I could either answer or spend the next fifteen minutes hearing about her contented marriage, their plans for a baby, or worse, help brainstorm a hotel incentive to entice travelers to the Waterfront. *No, thank you.*

"Hunter. His name is Hunter." I tilted my chin toward her and did my best not to smile. *Hunter.*

"Hunter… what?"

"Uh…." I dropped my head back and stared into a starless sky. "*Ay Dios mio*, I forgot to get his last name." The guy's eyes were a mixture of green and brown that whirled together and spun me for a loop. "After I got his luggage, I never asked for his name and I assumed he's staying here, but I'm not a hundred percent. I guess I got distracted."

"*Ah, yeah.* Carmen's sweet on someone." Katie elbowed me. "Aren't ya, aren't ya?"

"You're as *loca* as your husband."

"Bogart? You love Bogart. He's your buddy."

"Yeah, yeah, yeah, Bogart's my buddy. So are you, but—" I scratched my neck. "—none of that's going to matter when Richard realizes I have keys to a Mercedes, a bag with the bellhop, and no guest to charge the parking to."

She wrapped her arm around me. "That's why you're *so* lucky we're friends."

I glanced at Katie, and her dark brown eyes practically danced. "Qué estás hablando?"

"Mi español es pequeño."

"Not bad for a gringa."

"Great, so now that we've agreed I know very little Spanish… I got the '*qué*' part of what you said. But nothing else."

"I asked, 'What are you talking about?'"

"Ah." She smiled. "You forget, *amiga*, that as the new Assistant Public Relations and Marketing Director, I have access to the most coveted tool in the hotel."

"*Que bruto!* That's disgusting. I don't want to hear again about how you and Bogart hung a maintenance sign on a room so you could make out." I shuddered. "Too much information."

She swatted my arm. "I'm not talking about *Bogart's* tool!"

I giggled.

"I'm talking about the hotel's new software program, FrogKiss."

"FrogKiss? I just read an article about that in my IT class." I pushed my hat back, but it did little to ward off the sweat that beaded on my forehead. "It's great that we have the latest hotel software, but not sure how that's going to help. Richard's going to be back from his dinner break, and I've got a car with no guest attached to it. You know what a jerk he is. I've already been written up for being five minutes late because I was finishing a programming exam at school. Two more strikes, and I'm hasta la vista."

"Listen, that's not going to happen. The hotel is reimbursing part of your college tuition for you to get your degree in computer science. They don't make those kinds of investments lightly."

"Gracias. But we both know our IT department sucks." I quickly raised a finger. "With the exception of Georgina."

"True, but Georgina is only one person. That's why the hotel hired an outside contractor."

"Was this person responsible for loading the FrogKiss software?"

"No." Katie smiled. "I think the guy that's here is actually the *developer*. Like it's his baby, or frog."

I shook my head. "Qué? Why would you think that? Did his bag have a giant frog on it?" I elbowed her. "Although, the FrogKiss logo does have a really cute frog wearing a golden crown. As you would say, 'Totes adorb.'"

Katie laughed. "No, it wasn't his bag. I haven't even seen him. It was the fact that Michael kept asking the front desk attendants if his frog guy was in-house yet." She paused. "And Michael's usually not one to do the asking. He's more likely to ask his bubble-headed assistant to do it for him."

"So, based on that you think he's the developer of FrogKiss? What am I missing?"

"Nothing. It's just a hunch."

"Well, if you end up finding out who this Frog man is, point him in my direction. I'd love to meet the genius behind FrogKiss." I shook my head. "Okay, we've got to focus. Put your hunches and FrogKiss to good use and find me the room number for Hunter," I said.

"I've only used the software once, so hopefully I can remember each step. Although it was pretty easy," Katie said.

"I read that the software is *amazing*. It finds exactly what you're looking for, with the least possible information, without the trial and error of looking for the right person, but finding the wrong one." I came up for air. "You know why the developer called it FrogKiss, don't you?"

Katie shook her head. "Nope. No clue."

"Oh, it's really great. The idea is that instead of kissing

a bunch of frogs while searching for a prince, the software finds exactly who you're looking for on the first try." Whenever I spoke about computers, writing code, and programming, I felt like I could talk forever. There was never a language barrier with computers—coding was universal. "That's actually their slogan, 'FrogKiss—We'll find who you're looking for.' Clever, right?"

"Ah, you're turning into a computer nerd." Katie tilted her head and smiled at me.

I replied by rolling my eyes.

"Well, Miss Programmer, if you know how great the software is, then you know that it's the answer to your problem."

"I think." I rubbed my neck. "But it's for guests who check in, right? And I'm not sure Hunter checked in. I left his bag with the bellhop and…." *Did he go to the front desk?* I drew a blank.

"Let me guess. You were too busy watching him walk away that you didn't notice if he checked in?"

This time I couldn't hide my smile. "He did have a great ass."

"You and men's butts."

"I do like a good ass. And his was—" I slowly inhaled and on the exhale the word flowed from my lips. "—perfect."

"Then we *have* to find Mr. Hunter with the perfect ass," she said.

"I read that FrogKiss does cut down the time."

"You're not kidding me," Katie said, "since we no longer have to spend *hours* searching through hundreds of registrations in *hopes* of finding a guest that used his first name and not just his first initial, this new software truly is a prince. There's no more scouring the land of online registrations trying to find the right guest on the very last search. We find it on the first search. So, happily ever after is now one keystroke away," she said.

"So, we can access *any* guest, even if we only have his first name?"

"I only need his first initial."

"Listen, I'm all about technological advancements, but that seems *waaay* too good to be true," I said.

Katie wagged a finger. "Don't be a hater. It works. We had a guest arrive without any proper identification—no driver's license or passport. I was called to the front desk to assist. Apparently, this guest was chauffeured to the property from her Malibu home and assumed we'd recognize her."

"Was she some movie star?"

"Uh, yeah, like thirty years ago. I quickly googled her and even her photos were outdated. But, still, for security and privacy reasons, we needed some sort of proof that Mrs. Smith was really Mrs. Smith. But she wasn't sure if her personal assistant or her regular driver made the reservation for her weekend stay, and of course, she didn't know the last names of either of her employees," Katie rolled her eyes, "so we were left with simply an initial for each employee: D and M. Daryon, the personal assistant and Max, her regular driver."

"And from those initials you were able to find her reservation?"

Katie slowly nodded. "Legit. FrogKiss allows you to enter an initial in either the first or last name field and then it spits out possibilities."

"That's crazy," I said.

"Her room and the online security questions that FrogKiss provides the guest that only they could answer. And while this woman may be an open book, she's got more pages than a library. I'm *really not* interested in how many lovers she's had, which was one of the questions someone chose for her security profile." Katie shuddered, and I laughed. "Of course, the software works faster if the guest is already checked in, but even if they're not and have a pending reservation, it'll work because we enter info into a specific field for those queries."

"That's awesome. Let's just hope Hunter checked in." I hooked my arm beneath her arm. "*Vamonos!* We've got some frogs to kiss."

CHAPTER **THREE**

"Hunter!" His silver Armani suit with its custom tailoring made him look like he belonged back on Wall Street, not in a relaxed beachfront hotel suite.

"Michael." I shook his outstretched hand. "How's the new software working out?"

He nodded toward the chair beside the desk. "Well, that's the thing, Hunter, FrogKiss is *very* efficient. But"—his eyes darkened—"while I want our staff to be able to access information more quickly, I'm afraid the new software has created a dilemma for our directors."

I glanced at the laptop positioned between us. "I see. What's the hiccup?" I avoided saying "problem," because it's a word Michael Harpington would pounce upon.

"Can I be frank?"

Dude, for what you're paying me, you can be Frank, Sammy, Dino, and the entire Rat Pack, I don't care. "Absolutely. What's going on?"

"As you know, the Waterfront Point has a myriad of

VIPs staying at the resort."

I nodded.

"And it's imperative that none of the staff are able to search for fake names of VIPs staying at the resort to sell to tabloids. A-list stars and Washington elite frequent our property quite regularly, but they never book under their own names for privacy purposes."

"Of course."

"So, the Director of Rooms wanted a way to make sure A-listers using the resort will be ensured anonymity while staying at the Point."

"Perfectly understood. I can install an update that conceals the real identity of the guest that's password protected for your director's eyes only." I was about to sit back in the chair, but realized from the squint in Michael's eyes that he had a larger bomb to drop.

"Actually, along that line of password protection, is there…?" He steepled his fingers. "How do I say this?"

I gave him a dead-fish-eye stare, revealing nothing, but looking blankly at the soulless troll across from me.

"Hunter, with this new software you've developed, we aren't able to track our employees' time and how it's being spent, which is what I thought was an option when we purchased it from you."

What the fuck? He must have me confused with George Orwell. I'm supposed to convert—or rather pervert—my software into some Big Brother employee tracking device? I suppose he also expects me to goose-step to his fascism too? Hell, no. Instead, I slowly nodded as if I were lost in thought, when really I was trying to mentally remember the wording of the contract I entered into with Big Brother. *How long am I on the hook with this dirtbag?*

"Our Director of Finance was fairly certain that with our one-year contract, updates were included?"

Bastard. "Of course updates like password protection for A-list guests are included. I was just trying to conceptualize the best way to go about this new *upgrade*, which isn't included in the contract." *Game. Set. Match, asshole. If I'm going to install a monitor for you to check on your employees, people like Carmen, then it's going to cost you.*

"An upgrade, I see." His fingers were long, bony, and white. It was like watching the Grim Reaper play Itsy Bitsy Spider. Eventually he placed them on the desk between us and firmly patted the mahogany finish. "That's fine. Just fine. After you upgrade the software on this visit, include it in your monthly invoice."

I curtly smiled. "Absolutely."

"Excellent, excellent. I was going to invite you to dinner, but with all I've placed before you, it looks like your plate's rather overflowing." His white teeth and bleached blond hair were a startling contrast to his fake baked skin that gave him an almost orange hue. "From reviewing FrogKiss, I see that you're checked in. Please enjoy all the amenities, including room service, while you're a guest of the Waterfront."

I nodded. "Thank you, I will."

He cupped his knees and stood. "Then I'll leave you to it."

I rose and stood toe to toe with him. "Until next time,"

I said.

When the door closed behind him, I shut the hotel's laptop, pulled out mine, and plugged in a thumb drive.

"So, he wants to watch his staff. Sure, no problem, as long as I can watch him." My fingers flew across the keyboard, writing code, creating a password-protected file for Michael to use at his discretion. But before I finished, I entered the dark web to create a link that couldn't be traced—at least not by the hotel's IT staff. It would allow me to record the user of the password protected account's activity. Anytime they logged, surveyed, or creeped on their staff, I'd know.

To test my code, I needed someone on the staff who'd be willing to break the rules. And I knew just the girl.

CHAPTER **FOUR**

"It's got to be him, right?" Katie hovered over my shoulder. I shrugged; she was so close, she had become my shadow. But to be fair, I was sitting behind her desk using her executive password to access the check-in log.

"I don't see any other Hunter listed," I said, with my focus fixed on her laptop.

"Hunter Hughes." She nudged me. "Sounds rich."

I pointed toward the screen and followed my finger across to the room assigned to Hunter Hughes. "Twelfth floor, fancy."

"Nah."

The tone of her voice made me glance in her direction.

"Now if he was on the concierge floor, that'd be fancy. But he's far from the top," Katie said.

"You're *loca*. There's only fifteen floors in the hotel."

"Yes, but the top *two* are on the concierge level." She leaned into me and her wavy, out-of-control hair clung to me like ivy overtaking a trellis.

"Your husband's right. Your hair is like Chewbacca's." I licked my lips, pretty sure her fur had stuck to my gloss. "What are you looking for?"

"Why Hunter was placed on the twelfth floor." Her eyes narrowed, and then her mouth contorted. "Well, that makes sense. Mr. Harpington always puts his guests on that floor."

"Where do you see that?" I glanced at the system data that was itemized by a code I wasn't as familiar with.

"See the MH next to the billing icon?"

I followed the billing column that concluded with the owner's initials. "So that means what?"

"It means all the billing charges go to Mr. Harpington's account."

"What would Hunter do to be a guest of Mr. Harpington?"

Katie raised her shoulders and her blondish-brown hair threatened to coat me again. "Not sure. Mr. Harpington comps a lot of rooms."

"Qué?"

"A lot of them are corporate giveaways. Like he offers a room stay for charity events that people bid on," she said.

I slowly nodded and glanced around her office. It was smaller than a cubicle, more like a broom closet with a sublet. Still, it had a door, which apparently made it an office. With that logic, the bedroom I rented in my cousin Julia's house was my home office. Katie's door was open with a view to the front of the hotel. The only sound from the lobby was the rubber wheels on Tomás's electrical cart, which screeched against the marble. He pushed the cart from one light fixture to another. Tomás was my cousin's son. I was closer in age to him than I was with his mom, but he'd always be little Tomás to me. He glanced in our direction and tipped his head like he was cool.

"Carmen, just because Hunter is a guest of Mr. Harpington that doesn't necessarily mean that he won some raffle. Though if he bid on it, he bid high. Our room packages aren't cheap—especially at an auction where rich people like to show off by outbidding its value. Rich white people, am I right?"

I laughed. "Yeah, sure, because with your new raise and Bogart's house, you're really hurting there, *gringa*."

"Fair enough."

"So only people who've won a bid stay on the twelfth floor?"

She shook her head, and I leaned away. Katie's hair could have its own zip code for the space it consumed. "No, Hunter could be a guest of Mr. Harpington for some business they're working on."

She pushed me out of her seat. "Let me see if there are any notes."

I moved over, and she moved in.

I glanced at the data and spotted a notes section, which was off to the side of the guest check-in information. The home zip code listed beside Hunter's name was 97366.

"Where does he live?" I pointed toward his mailing address, which only revealed his zip code. "I don't recognize that."

"Hmm… me neither." Katie clicked open another tab on her computer and ran a quick Internet search. A picture of a navy-and-white schooner on glassy water surfaced, along with the city and state. "Newport, Oregon. Huh. Looks pretty."

"Yeah, it does."

"Okay, let's go back and look at his notes section."

"What's kept in there again?"

"Notes about each guest. Like if a guest prefers one bottled water to another, we note it here. Or perhaps if a friend is staying with them during their visit."

"A friend?"

"You know, a *friend*." Katie's eyebrows waggled as if that should clear things up.

I pursed my lips together. "No clue what you're talking about, *amiga*."

"Suffice to say, the Point Resort wants to ensure we don't refer to someone as 'Mrs.' when perhaps they're simply a female friend or companion accompanying a guest."

"<u>*Ay caramba*</u>. Does the guest know we keep all this personal info on them?"

Katie shot me a look that quickly reminded me that when it came to the Waterfront Point Resort, certain rules of conduct didn't apply. "We also keep food allergies in this section."

"Sure, because the only person that should kill the guest is the missus, and not a stray peanut."

Katie chuckled. "Which is why our notes section is so important."

"So... does Mr. Hughes have a *friend*?"

Katie clicked open the tab into his file and burst out laughing. "No, but his favorite food is Mexican."

"Ha ha ha. It does not say that."

She nodded. "Yes. It does." Her red manicured nail tapped the screen. "Ah, yah, he likes him a little chimichanga. Something a little dark and spicy." Her dark eyebrows did that annoying dance when she was excited, and her arms flapped like a chicken. The girl was crazy as hell, but I loved her. Of course, I'd never admit it, because then she'd want to spend more time together.

"Chimichangas are Tex-Mex," I said flatly. "If he truly liked Mexican food, then there would have been *antojitos* listed in his file."

"Waaaeell, la-de-frickin'-da. We've got ourselves an expert on Mexican food."

I rolled my eyes, but still laughed. "I'm an expert, Katie, because I'm *Mexican.*"

"You don't have to bring race into it, sheesh." She grinned. "So, what are anti-o-fritos?"

"Aunt-toe-he-toes. It's street food sold by vendors at small traditional markets in Mexico. Long before the food truck craze, there were street vendors peddling *antojitos*. It literally means 'little cravings.'"

Katie practically fell out of her seat. "Little cravings?"

"*Pinche gringa.* Sometimes a word is just a word."

She waggled her eyebrows at me. "Sure. Whatever you say." Katie tapped the screen so hard I thought she was going to leave an indent. "Well, if Mr. Hunter Hughes does have any *little cravings* tonight, he just happens to have a king-size bed in his room."

"Great. I'll keep that in mind." I squinted at the small type in the notes section. "Does it say what his business is?"

Katie's eyes got as large as quarters. "Oh my God!"

"Shhh!" I glanced toward the foyer. "What?"

"Hunter *is* the FrogKiss developer!"

I smacked her arm. "No way."

"Way. It has his title and occupation. Hunter Hughes, Founder & Chairman FrogKiss, Inc."

"*Damn.* Didn't see that coming."

"I had a hunch, but that's all it was, a hunch," Katie said.

Stunned, I stared at his title that looked almost as impressive as the man. "I can't believe I just met the developer of FrogKiss. He's so young."

"Right. I only saw him briefly, but he wasn't some scrawny, geeked-out nerd man."

"No, he wasn't."

Katie glanced up from her computer, and we both saw Richard, my supervisor, walking toward her office.

"Shit," I said under my breath.

"I'll stall the Dick. Park the car, and I'll charge it to room 1225."

"I already parked it," I said, just before Richard crossed the threshold into Katie's office that barely fit her and her desk, let alone two extra bodies.

Katie's fingers quickly keyed in the code for overnight parking that looked like "OV" and the Enter key. As much as I wanted to learn the software ins and outs, Richard and his furrowed forehead, dark eyes, and unrelenting stare kept my eyes straight forward.

"Hey, Richard, finished your meal break?" I said, avoiding using dinner or lunch, which annoyed the hell outta him. *It's four o'clock in the afternoon, why would I be having dinner? It's a meal break, Gonzalez.* He rarely, if ever, called me by my first name, which suited me just fine. I always called him by his first name because it reminded me what a dick he was.

"Yes. Imagine finishing my meal break to return to the front drive where only one of my valets is on duty."

"Actually, Richard." Katie rose. "I paged Ms. Gonzalez."

"Oh, is that so? And why would the Assistant Public Relations and Marketing Director require a valet?"

"Because, Richard, one of Mr. Harpington's guests changed rooms, and I had to ensure that his car was as well taken care of as he."

Richard's face evened out into his perpetual scowl. "Oh, I see."

Katie didn't back down. "I'm so glad that serving Mr. Harpington and his guests meets your approval, Richard."

He slightly bowed his head in acknowledgement of the verbal scolding. "Are you through with Ms. Gonzalez?"

"In a bit. I was showing her how to adjust a billing charge in the event her supervisor is ever off on a meal break. Cross-training, as you know, is something Mr. Harpington has been very vocal about implementing at the resort."

He slowly nodded.

"We were just beginning. I've got about another hour if we want Carmen to know the new software update, or at least what we know of it. So...," Katie glanced at the computer and up to Richard, "about an hour."

Richard glanced at the oversized watch on his wrist.

"It's eight now. Her shift ends in two hours."

Katie arched her eyebrows in feigned surprise. Like she didn't know when my shift ended. Hell, every week she made sure my work schedule didn't interfere with my class schedule. She may be crazy, but she was loyal, and that meant everything to me. "Well…." Katie paused. "I suppose I could message Mr. Harpington that you need Carmen back for the latter part of her shift…." She purposefully let her voice trail off.

The girl is good.

"No, that won't be necessary." He made eye contact with me. "Gonzalez, clock off promptly at ten. No overtime."

"Absolutely," I said.

Richard turned and practically marched out of Katie's office.

"Ass," Katie said, resuming her seat behind her desk.

"Wow. You played that well."

Her brown eyes flicked up at me. "Listen, Richard's a holdover from the old management that wasn't working at the Point Resort when we picketed the property for equal working conditions. I'm not about to go back on all the progress we made, especially with the likes of Richard Hobbs, who still believes that a woman's place isn't in the front of the house unless," she held up her hand to stop my objection, "it's to park cars or clean the outside windows."

"Agreed."

"So, the fact that I'm actually an equal with him in terms of position and rank at the hotel, well, that's got to drive him batshit."

"Yeah, it does." I paused. "But you bring up a good point. You're both equal rank at the hotel. So, doesn't that mean he has the same access to the computer and FrogKiss that you do? Won't he be able to see that Hunter never changed rooms?"

"Yes, but before Dick came in, I not only added in Hunter's parking, but I temporarily switched his rooms. If he doesn't want to move, I can switch it back and no one will be the wiser. It's in a hold right now. If Richard looked, he'd see Hunter in two rooms, which is how we do it until the guest is out of one room and into another. Of course, Mr. Hughes doesn't know any of this yet, but he will." Katie leaned back in her chair. "First, let's kill time in my office so you don't have to return to front drive hell and I don't have to stare at my computer hoping a marketing program will suddenly materialize. Then we'll go see Hunter." Her lips curved into a smile. "It'll be fun to meet *the* FrogKiss man. Maybe he's the prince you've been waiting for?"

CHAPTER **FIVE**

"Listen, I've got this." I dipped a boneless buffalo wing into the stainless steel round cup filled with barbeque sauce, and popped it in my mouth.

"Brother, I'm sure you do, but that doesn't mean I can't be concerned."

"Concern noted. But even you have to agree that what this bastard Michael wants to do is bullshit." I reached for another wing from the mountain of deliciousness that room service delivered.

"Yah… but weren't you the one that some construction company hired to find out who was accessing certain records?"

"When did your mind start logging what I did?"

I heard my brother's hearty chuckle and it made me smile.

"Hunter, I may not know any useful facts or figures, but I have a very good memory of very bad things. And it's logged enough about you to build a cabin. So maybe this hotel guy isn't as ethical as you'd like, but he's not breaking the law, is he?"

I paused with a wing drowned in tangy barbeque. Had Michael asked me to break any law? I flung the wing in my mouth and chewed on it for a while before I answered. "No. He's not breaking any law. It's just not kosher."

"Yah, but you've done it before with that eff tail program you have."

This time I laughed. "It's not any program I created, but damn, brother, your memory is solid. It's called tailing the file, or tail minus f, because that's the command line—minus f for follow, because you're basically installing a program that writes to a file so when those half-wits at the construction company accessed confidential records, I could monitor their activity in real time."

"So, what's the difference with what this Michael douche asked you to do?"

I dropped another wing into sauce. "He's not tailing a file to see if employees are accessing information they shouldn't. He wants to know what people are doing online. There's a big difference."

"So, tail him. Add that program on and monitor his activity."

"Already did." I patted the thumb drive on the lanyard around my neck and visualized the hotel key I left in the glovebox of my rental car. "And I added another level of security off-site to cover my ass."

"Nice work!"

I smiled. "Thanks, big brother. 'Preciate that," I said

with a mouthful of barbeque.

"What the hell are you eating?"

"Wings." I could practically see my brother smile. "I'm going to win that prize next year."

"Bro, you've got to let it go."

"And pass up a thousand dollars and a plate full of wings? Hell no. The Newport chicken-eating contest is mine. I'm going to own that bitch. In fact…." I grabbed three wings off the plate, bobbed them in barbeque, and popped them in my mouth. I chewed quickly and swallowed, but something got stuck. I tried to clear my throat, but the food wouldn't go down. I grabbed the glass of water.

"Hunter? You still there?"

I nodded and drank, but it wouldn't dislodge the wing. Panic gripped me. I couldn't breathe. I dropped the phone and hit my chest with my fist. Nothing. I hit harder. *Fuck. What the hell.* I rammed my stomach against the edge of the desk, knocking over my laptop and sending food flying. But any attempt to dislodge the chunk failed. *Oh my God.*

I reached for the phone beside my bed and dialed 911, but the only sound I heard was a fast busy signal. *Fuck. What's the code to get an outside line?* I felt dizzy and couldn't focus on the instructions beside the phone.

Suddenly a knock sounded at my door. I clamored toward it and reached for the handle, barely getting it open. *Carmen.*

CHAPTER **SIX**

"Hunter!" I screamed, and darted toward him. He slumped to the floor. His face was dusky and his lips were a light shade of blue. I looked at his shirt to see if his chest was rising and falling. It wasn't. I leaned over him and placed my ear between his mouth and nose and listened for breathing sounds. There weren't any.

"Oh my God. He's not breathing." I glanced at the room service tray on the floor. Chicken wings scattered across the carpet. "Katie, I think he's choking. Call 911."

Katie hopped over me to the bedside phone. I heard her punch in a series of numbers to access an outside line. "Yes. It's an emergency. A man isn't breathing. Yes, he's unconscious. Carmen."

I looked at her.

"Okay, uh, she said to check his airway to see if there's anything visible."

I knelt in front of him, gently opened his mouth and leaned back out of the shadows to get a better look. "I think… there's a… chicken wing?"

"She thinks there's a chicken wing," Katie said into the phone. "Carmen, reach a finger into his mouth and try to…."

My legs shook, my hands began to sweat, and adrenaline coursed through my body. I glanced at Katie, who was nodding into the phone.

"Yeah, okay, put your finger in his mouth and try to sweep out the blockage."

I gently placed my finger in his mouth.

"Wait!" Katie screamed, and I seized. My body tensed, my jaw clenched, and I felt like I was going to throw up.

"Be careful not to push the food deeper into his throat, um, I mean, airway."

I held my breath as if air would cause the wing to move further down his throat. I carefully reached back into his mouth toward the edge of the chicken wing, but I couldn't get a good hold of it. "Katie, there's just a tip and my finger keeps slipping."

Katie relayed the information. "Start CPR."

I heard her, but I froze. For all the emergency training the hotel had provided, my brain went blank. Hunter wasn't breathing, and I couldn't remember how to perform CPR. *Come on, Carmen—not now. There's no time. You can do it.*

I bowed my head and quickly said a prayer. "Ayudame, Señor."

Suddenly, three words surfaced. *Call. Pump. Blow.* The takeaway from my CPR training. *Thank you, God.* I tilted his head slightly and lifted his chin. *Call.* Katie had called 911. *Pump.* I placed my hands, one on top of the other, in the middle of his chest, but there was something bumpy. I lifted his shirt. A thumb drive was in the middle of his hairless chest. I tried to tear off the lanyard, but it wouldn't tear. I fumbled, but managed to unclip it, tuck it in my uniform pants pocket, and used my body weight to push hard and fast against his chest in rapid succession. I looked around the hotel room for a clock. The one on the nightstand was turned toward the wall. *Dammit.* I began counting, and when a minute passed, I pinched his nose shut and placed my mouth over his.

Blow. I blew into his mouth to make his chest rise, but it didn't.

"What am I doing wrong? His chest isn't rising like it's supposed to."

The 911 operator must have heard me, because Katie immediately said. "Re-tilt his head and see if you can remove the object."

The chicken wing hadn't moved. I reached into his mouth and tried to grab it, but it kept slipping away. "I need plyers! Or tweezers. Something! I can't get a hold on it." I brushed my hands on my black pants and tried again, but the wing was slippery, and when I pulled my hand out, it was red.

"Oh my God! Katie!" I showed her my hand, streaked in what had to be blood.

"There's blood in his throat," Katie said into the phone. "Go back to chest compressions, the EMT should be here any second."

I wiped my hands on my pants and pressed down on his

chest with all my might, but he didn't respond. His chest didn't rise and fall. *Come on, Hunter, just breathe. Please. Just a little breath. You can do this.*

"Recheck his mouth!" Katie yelled.

The blue from his lips had spread to his face. *Why isn't it working? What am I doing wrong?* I pushed the thoughts out of my mind and reached into his mouth for the chicken remnants. This time I got an edge and yanked hard. A red, slimy chunk of chicken pulled free.

"I got it!" I held the wing high.

But Hunter still didn't respond.

"Chest compressions." Katie dropped the phone and appeared beside me. She began pressing her weight into him, pumping hard and fast—but no response.

The door to the hotel room swung open and the Director of Security, Bill Clark, was dressed in a city league baseball uniform. *What time is it?* Mr. Clark quickly moved aside for two emergency medical technicians that rushed toward Hunter. They pushed past me and took over for Katie.

"We got the chicken wing out, but he's not breathing," I said. My plea fell silent as the men in crisp white uniforms worked in tandem on Hunter.

"Why isn't he breathing?" I asked.

"We're doing everything we can. How long has he been unresponsive?"

I looked at Katie, whose face was as blank as my memory of time. "I don't know… maybe four, five minutes?" she said.

"Yeah, probably four or five minutes," I said.

"A lack of oxygen—" The man stopped midsentence when his coworker, who affixed something to Hunter, shook his head.

"Is he dead?" Katie's voice shook.

The men exchanged a glance, and I knew.

"Okay, he's bagged," one of them said.

A bag stuck out of Hunter's mouth. As one EMT performed CPR, the other one manually pressed the bag, force-feeding air into his lungs. When Hunter's chest began to rise and fall, my hand went to my chest. *He's breathing. He's not dead.*

A third man arrived with a gurney. The room buzzed with activity and voices as the three men squatted in front of Hunter.

"Let's do this together," one of them said as they gently lifted him onto the steel gurney that looked cold, sterile, and uncomfortable.

The General Manager, Mr. Adams, and the Director of Security, Mr. Clark, stood off to the side. They briefly made eye contact with me and Katie, but their focus remained on Hunter.

"Jerry, he's a guest of Mr. Harpington," I heard Mr. Clark tell Mr. Adams.

"Oh Jesus." Mr. Adams rubbed his forehead. "Okay, I'll contact Michael." He glanced at Katie. "Kandy's still out on vacation, can you handle the press?"

Katie nodded.

Mr. Adams turned to me. "Not a word about this to anyone." His tone was sharp, but as he took a step toward me it changed. He went from talking at me to talking to me. Still, the way he approached me pissed me off. He spoke slowly and enunciated his words, as if I didn't comprehend English. Worse, he had to look at my name tag to know who I was.

"Carmen, we want to get ahead of this situation because it's the best thing to do for our guests in protecting his privacy."

Really? *That's your biggest priority? Bad publicity?* My adrenaline was already spiked, but Mr. Adams made it soar.

"So, until Ms. Bogart can draft a press release, I have to ask that you don't share this with anyone—other staff, your family or friends. Does that make sense?"

I took a step toward him. "English may be my second language, but I still write, speak, and understand it far better than—"

Katie gently placed her hand on my shoulder. She knew me well, and keying off at the General Manager probably wasn't a smart move.

"Of course you understand everything," Mr. Adams said with a forced smile on his face. "There's just a lot going on, and I know sometimes in emergency situations we tend to react versus taking a beat to breathe."

I had been so consumed with trying to get Hunter to breathe that I couldn't remember the last time I had. I watched as he was wheeled away with a bag breathing for him, and Mr. Clark running in front of the EMTs to access the service elevator. I didn't know what to do. I walked toward the desk, slid down the wall, and sat on the carpet in

Hunter's hotel room. Katie huddled beside me.

Mr. Adams glanced at us. "That's a good idea. Collect your thoughts and take a minute."

When he closed the door behind us, the room was unnervingly still.

"Hunter! Hunter!"

I turned to Katie. "Did you hear that?"

We listened. "Hunter!"

"Is someone in the bathroom?" Katie jumped up and ran to the bathroom. "No one's in here."

His name rang in the room. "Hunter!"

I listened and headed toward the sound. *The bed*. I pulled the duvet aside and spotted an iPhone that I immediately placed to my ear. "Hello?"

"What happened to Hunter?"

"Who is this?" I asked.

"I'm his brother. Who is this?"

"Carmen."

"Is my brother okay?"

My head lowered and tears flowed down my face. "I don't know. I did everything I could."

CHAPTER **SEVEN**

The six o'clock local news led with the story. "A twenty-six-year-old man is in critical condition after apparently choking on a chicken wing at the Waterfront Point Resort in Huntington Beach this evening."

So much for getting ahead of it. Or perhaps this was the Point getting ahead of it. I couldn't think straight. My cousin Julia handed me a shot of tequila, and my *abuelita* gently kissed the top of my head.

"You did more than anyone could expect, *mija.*" My grandmother's voice soothed my frayed nerves, but the tequila deadened them. "I'll light a candle for you and for this young man at church."

"Hunter," I said, with tears tugging at the corners of my eyes. "His name is Hunter."

"Well, I'll light a candle for you and Hunter."

I smiled softly. My grandmother believed all of life's troubles could be cured by lighting a candle at church. If it meant Hunter would be okay, I'd light them all.

"My prayer group is saying a *novena*," Julia added.

After her husband, Juan Carlos, walked out on her and their son, serving her with divorce papers, Julia followed the path of any devout Catholic. She applied for an annulment on grounds that her husband was ignorant about the nature of marriage, which was actually a legit Catholic canon. Juan Carlos was ignorant. He just didn't believe that marriage was a permanent relationship between a man and a woman. Add insult to injury, his only interest in procreating was with women other than his wife. As a result, the church granted Julia an annulment and the courts awarded her custody of Tomás. She returned to the fold at Our Lady of Perpetual Help and joined their divorced catholic support group. Our abuelita was certain my return to the church was imminent, and with what happened today, she may be right.

"Nine days of prayers. Oh, mija, what a gift," she said, patting my hand. She then looked at my cousin. "That's very sweet of you, *muneca.*"

Julia and I didn't have to vie for our grandmother's attention—she had her own term of endearment for each of us. She called Julia *muneca*, which means doll. And mija was a combination of *mi hija*, which meant my daughter.

Hunter was someone's *hijo* and *hermano*. He was a son and a brother. What was his family nickname? Who was praying for him?

CHAPTER **EIGHT**

"Mr. and Mrs. Hughes, I realize you've traveled all day and into the night to be here and…." The doctor paused. "I wish I had better news to give you."

I stood beside my parents in the shadow of their grief. Hunter was in a hospital bed not ten feet from us. I still couldn't make myself look in the direction of my little brother. Numbness had worked its way through my body, but it hadn't deadened my heart that ached. *Oh, Hunter, man. What'd you do?*

"When your son arrived to us yesterday, he had already lost oxygen to his brain."

The doctor wasn't much older than my parents. Had to be in his midsixties. His dark hair had streaks of gray, and the deep, inset wrinkles beneath his eyes didn't look like they were caused from the California sun, but rather his profession.

"The brain is extremely sensitive to a lack of oxygen and will begin to die within four to six minutes without it," he said. "We don't know how long Hunter went without oxygen. We spoke to one woman at the hotel who called 911 while her colleague administered CPR, and she wasn't sure how long they worked on him before the paramedics arrived. However, from the absence of brain activity, Hunter went without oxygen long enough to cause irreversible brain death."

"But his heart is still beating." My mom's teary voice felt like a punch to the stomach.

The doctor slowly nodded. "It can be very confusing for families. Someone who is brain dead may appear alive— they may have a heartbeat, they may look like they're breathing, their skin may still be warm to the touch. But there is no life when brain activity ceases."

"So, he's in a coma?" my father asked.

The doctor shook his head before he answered. "No. A coma means that a person still has some brain activity."

"And Hunter's brain doesn't...." My dad suddenly looked down at the linoleum tile in the hospital room.

"That's correct," he said.

"How can you be sure?" Mom's voice teetered on panic.

"There are tests we run to determine brain activity."

"Maybe he's just in a coma, like my husband said," my mom said.

"I understand that it can be confusing," the doctor said. "But the primary difference between someone in a coma and someone who is brain dead is that when someone is in a coma they still have some brain activity. When someone is brain dead, they don't."

My parents looked more confused than before.

"The essential difference is that Hunter's brain no longer helps him function." The doctor used language they seemed to understand.

"But his heart is still beating," Mom protested.

"Some functions, like a heartbeat, may linger. But without brain function, Hunter's body will eventually shut down. He cannot breathe on his own," he said.

"But his heart…." My mom wasn't one to give up on her kids.

I bit the inside of my mouth, but the pain cut too deep. I gently placed my arm around her.

"Mom, I'm so sorry," I said.

Tears streamed down her cheeks when she looked up at me. "Hank, how can this be? I just spoke to your brother."

I nodded.

"Is there any surgery that you can do?" My father resumed eye contact with the doctor, who again slowly shook his head.

"There isn't any surgical procedure that will reverse your son's brain death. I'm terribly sorry. I can't imagine your loss."

"Maybe his brain just needs time to heal," my mom said.

My hold on her tightened as I spoke into the side of her head. "Mom, that's not what Hunter would have wanted. To be kept alive on a machine that's breathing for him. That's not who Hunter was."

Her body shook against me. "I can't. I can't say goodbye. He's my baby. He's my youngest."

"I know, Mom. He's my kid brother, and I should've done more to protect him."

My father's laughter startled us both. "He had a mouthful of chicken wings." He shook his head. "I don't know how many he stuffed in his mouth, but…." His voice trailed off and he brushed the back of his bald head. "That's something Hunter would've done. The kid was always putting things in his mouth, from the time he was born." Tears brimmed in my father's graying eyes. "Martha, we can't keep our boy like that." His voice cracked and he briefly looked over at my brother lying in the hospital bed. "That's no way to live. He deserves better."

"He deserves to be alive," my mom said, moving out of my embrace and into my father's open arms. Her cries filled the room, even drowning the drone of the machine that breathed for my brother. "George, I want him to be alive. I want my baby to be okay. I just want him back."

"We all do, but the Hunter we love isn't there. That's just his body." My dad looked at the doctor over the top of my mom's head. "I know there must be some papers we have to sign in order to remove our son from life support."

My mom cried, sobbing in his arms.

"The order is at the nurses' station. I'll give you some time alone with your son." The lines beneath his eyes darkened with worry. "I'm *so* sorry for your loss." The door shut behind him as softly as an unspoken plea for forgiveness.

CHAPTER **NINE**

I stared at my iPhone, waiting for a text, call, or some update about Hunter. Instead the screen remained as black as the cloud that seemed to hang over me.

"That's it." I bolted off my bed, grabbed my car keys, and headed toward the front door. My feet felt heavy when I passed through the kitchen.

"Where you going?" Julia dipped a tortilla in red sauce and reached for the spoon propped in the pot of refried beans.

"I'm not sure. The hospital?" I shrugged. "I know the hotel was trying to be nice by giving me paid time off to 'regroup,' but not knowing what's going on with Hunter is not helping. The media's been silent about it ever since it first broke, which I'm sure is Katie doing her job, but the uncertainty is awful."

Julia sprinkled shredded chicken and cheese over the beans before she rolled the tortilla and placed it in the row of enchiladas that lined the large, rectangular adobe baking dish.

"That's got to be difficult." She wiped her forehead with the sleeve of her shirt. "Not knowing."

"It is. I just want to know one way or the other how he's doing."

Julia brushed her hands on the towel across her shoulder, and gently tucked my hair behind my ear. "Be careful. You and hospitals aren't the best of friends."

I swallowed the knot in my throat. "This is different."

"Okay." She reached for another corn tortilla from the stack on the stovetop. "I'm making your favorite." Her brown eyes danced with merriment.

"Gracias. It looks ah-mazing."

She laughed. "It will be." She shook the tortilla. "No llegues tarde por la cena."

"When am I ever late for dinner?"

"True." She blew a kiss in my direction, and I smiled.

The sixties rockabilly folk rock of the Beatles' "Nowhere Man" blast from the stereo in my rust-covered truck. I headed south toward Newport Beach and the coast highway. The closest hospital to the hotel was in Newport, where the ambulance took Hunter. The Beatles' melodic song about isolation and going nowhere aptly fit my mood.

The drive from Costa Mesa to Newport wasn't long enough. I pulled into the lot for emergency room parking, and found a spot close to the entrance. The doors slid open, with the information desk to the side.

"Hello." Her name tag read Betty, and she stood when I approached the desk. "May I help you?"

When Tomás worked maintenance at the hospital for a summer, he always spoke of the large section of senior volunteers referred to as "the Granny Nannies." Betty's white permed hair, large-framed glasses, and hot-pink smock filled with decorative pins and badges fit the bill. She smiled brightly and a "Save Lives—Donate Blood" pin flashed along with her teeth.

"A friend of mine was brought in two days ago by ambulance."

"And does your friend have a name?" The sincere curiosity in her eyes made it impossible to think she was being a smartass.

"Hughes. Hunter Hughes."

"Hughes?"

"Yes."

"Well, let's take a look." She sat behind her desk and peered over her glasses at the computer screen. The PC looked almost as old as Betty. *This is why I'll always find work.* Hospitals and businesses would always need upgrades. Nothing aged faster and became more obsolete quicker than technology.

"Hughes...." Betty moved the mouse by lifting it and then setting it back down on the desk—hard. The mouse was beaten down more times than a whack-a-mole. Betty was so proficient, she'd win every prize at the fair.

"Hunter. Okay, here he is." Her faded blue eyes scanned the screen. "All right. He's in neurology, which is in the south wing."

"Where is that? I only know the maternity wing from when my cousin had her baby, Tomás, but that was eighteen years ago and...." I glanced toward the elevators. "I think maternity was in here?"

"That's correct. It hasn't moved since the hospital changed ownership. Eighteen years ago it was a *county* hospital, you know."

Yup, that's why my cousin could afford it.

"Now it's *privately* owned." Her lips turned up in a smile that reminded me that the line between the haves and have nots in Orange County was only separated by time. A century ago, they couldn't give the land away. And now, on what used to be a lima bean farm, which I'd bet my paycheck was toiled by migrant workers, was the largest mall on the West Coast. South Coast Plaza may not have been built on the backs of my people, but it changed the landscape for them and of Orange County forever. From farmlands to hospitals, what had been open to all was now just open to a select few with deep enough pockets.

"Obstetrics is here in the East Tower. To get to neurology, you'll go past the infant care center to access the tunnel that'll lead you to the cancer and neurological centers."

"And is he there? Hunter?"

Betty's thick glasses couldn't mask her confusion. "Yes. He's listed as a patient."

He's not dead. My spirits suddenly lifted. "Great. Thank you."

I practically skipped toward the walkway. Artwork

hung on the walls leading to the tunnel, which was more of an archway that stretched across the hospital's main thoroughfare to the other wing.

The art varied, but was uniformly framed and matted in black and hung in symmetric precision on the wall. A red train drawn in crayon on a green hill that looked like an upside-down V caught my attention. Blue puffy clouds and a smiling sun with yellow lines shooting from its center touched the top of the red train. The drawing was signed by Ian, age three. *Was Ian a patient? And why did his train only make it halfway up the hill? Did he die before he reached the top?* My mind raced with morbid possibilities.

The next framed picture, of a rainbow, was drawn by Molly, age fifty-four. *Why would a fifty-four-year-old draw a rainbow? What was she hoping was on the other side? What was gold to her?*

Between Ian and Molly, the wall of pictures bummed me out. I focused on the blue signs that led me from the tunnel to the cancer center, where a fireplace was front and center. At the hotel we had a waterfall in the lobby to create ambiance. But a fireplace? *Ay caramba.* As if a cozy fire was going to make the reality of cancer better. *Stupid.* But if the faux fire didn't generate warmth, then the man tickling the ivories on a grand piano would. His playing was actually kind of nice. Soothing. When it came to hospitals, this was the concierge level.

Three grannies dressed in matching blue smocks clamored to greet me. "Hello! Are you checking in?"

"No." I backed away from them as if cancer were

contagious, when I knew from Mamá's breast cancer that it wasn't. Still, the sooner I could get out of the cancer center and into neurology, the better. Too many memories. Maybe if Mamá had been here, she'd have fared better.

A woman walked by me, tethered to a portable IV. Her skin was translucent and her sunken eyes stared vacantly from a gaunt face that had seen too much. But it was her patchy brown hair that made my chest deflate. *Oh, Mamá.* When she lost her beautiful brown hair, I wanted to shave my head in solidarity, but she wouldn't allow it.

"Mija, your hair is your crowning glory. When I see it, I see a brighter future."

The woman, clad only in a hospital gown, glanced in my direction. I smiled. She paused for a moment. I think it surprised her that I actually made eye contact with her and didn't gawk at the visible symptoms of her illness. *She is not her disease.* Something Mamá's battle taught me. The pang in my chest returned.

"So how can we help you?"

I resumed eye contact with the granny in the center. "I have a friend in neurology."

All three of the grannies' mouths formed perfect O's. Mouths agape, they pointed in the opposite direction of the fireplace and piano man. "That's just down the hallway."

The hallway from the cancer care center to neurology was tiled in marble. Still, for the expense, it felt too formal and worse, impersonal. I took a deep breath, but it did nothing to settle my nerves.

Instead of a granny, a nurse made eye contact with me

at the neurological station. A sign hung above her blonde head, Neurological Intensive Care.

"I'm here to see Hunter Hughes." I opted for bravado versus timidity. *Act as if.* Wasn't that what Julia always said? So I acted like I had every right to see him, when I had no right.

She didn't review the computer or the clipboard on the desk in front of her. She looked at me directly in the eye. "His family just left."

The finality in her tone made my eyes water.

"Did you know Hunter?"

I barely nodded.

"I think his family went to the chapel." She never broke eye contact with me. I knew the drill. Nurses knew everything. They were the ones, not the doctors, who stayed at the bedside of patients long after their shift ended. The role as communicator between Hunter's family and a total stranger was simply her way to protect her patient. She knew I didn't belong there. And if she had any reservations, my question confirmed it.

"Did he die?"

"I can't discuss patient history without the consent of the family." Hunter was as white as I was dark. The only way we were connected by family was by marriage, adoption, or a hospital mix-up.

"I understand." And I did. Still, that didn't stop the deluge of tears that streamed down my face. "I tried." For some reason, I wanted someone to know. "To save him. But...." My chest shook. "He wouldn't breathe, and I couldn't get the chicken...."

"Oh." Her voice dropped, and her blue eyes softened. "Were you one of the employees at the hotel? Are you Carmen?"

I nodded, but my face must have conveyed my confusion. *How does she know my name?*

She glanced at the clipboard. "The EMTs had Carmen Gonzalez and Katie Bogart on the report. I took a guess that you were Carmen."

A tear slipped down my cheek that I quickly brushed away.

The nurse looked in either direction and waved me toward the door in the nurses' station. She opened it, and I stood on the other side. "He's in room 232."

"Thank you."

"The family may not return, but if they do...."

"I understand." If Hunter's family returned, I was a trespasser.

I knew before I entered that he had passed. There wasn't any sound outside his hospital room. The blood pressure monitor that pushed out one steady beat after another was silent. The infusion pump that beeped when it ran out of a medication wasn't beep-beeping. The ventilator that sounded a warning when the patient moved or coughed was still. Nor were there any lights blinking their reflection against the small window beside the door. The one constant in Mamá's intensive care unit was the noise. The sheer volume of alarms hooked to her was overwhelming. She became desensitized to the constant bombardment of sound, but I never did. Anytime an alarm rang, my body seized. Was this the one? But when it happened and my sweet little Mamá drew her last breath, there was no sound, no alarm, no buzz. Her nurse had turned down the volume on the machines, and shut them off immediately afterward. A quiet hospital room can only mean one thing.

And if I doubted my experience or sixth sense that was on high alert, the telltale sign was that the nurse hadn't escorted me down the hall and into room 232. She had already said her goodbyes, and was now simply keeping watch.

I pushed hard to open the door and then entered softly. The tangle of cords that I imagined had been hooked to him were lassoed back on their machines.

His color wasn't much better than when I last saw him. He was no longer blue, but a gray pallor had settled on him, and I knew he would probably be cool to the touch.

"You just need a little light in here." I pulled the cord on the blinds and they rose.

But he didn't answer.

I quietly walked over to him.

"Hello." I tilted my head, but his friendly face didn't smile back. I carefully placed my hand on his chest, but my hand didn't rise and fall with his breath. "I'm *so* sorry."

I lowered my head and closed my eyes, but the pain cut through me. *I'm so sorry.*

###

She barely stood taller than my mom. In a pair of torn jeans, flip-flops, and T-shirt, she looked more relaxed and approachable than anyone I'd met in Newport. With her head lowered and her hair pulled back, her profile was as delicate as she was petite. Tears fell down cinnamon-colored cheeks.

"Her name's Carmen." Kelly walked up beside me outside my brother's room. I stood to the side of the window and watched. "She was one of the hotel employees who tried to save your brother."

I nodded. Her hand lay on my brother's chest like she was asking for his forgiveness, even though she was entirely blameless for what happened to him.

"I hope it was all right that I let her see Hunter." It was the first time I'd heard uncertainty from his nurse.

I looked at Kelly, who had cared for my brother as if her will and attention could pull him back from death when we all knew it couldn't. "Of course. Thank you."

She gently touched my shoulder. "If you need me, I'm just at the desk."

I barely smiled. "Thanks."

Kelly walked away, and I walked into my brother's room.

Carmen turned, and watery blue eyes pleaded for a different outcome. "I was just…." She glanced at my brother and her silky black ponytail shook. She made the sign of the cross and gently kissed his cheek. My mom had done the same thing. She walked toward me, and for once I wished I wasn't so tall. I wanted to stand eye to eye with her and give her the comfort she so desperately sought.

"I was just leaving." She tried to make a quick escape, but her flip-flops crossed paths with the wheel on Hunter's hospital bed.

I saw the fall before it happened. I reached for her, and when she tumbled forward she landed in my arms.

"¡Chinga tú madre, cabrón!" As soon as the words flew out, her hand covered her mouth. "Ay Dios mios."

"Are you okay?"

She barely made eye contact with me, choosing instead to nod.

"I'm not as fluent with Spanish as my brother is, I mean was." I swallowed. "But, uh, from the sound of it you really told that bed off."

Her smooth, flawless caramel skin tinged with a blush of red.

"I'm sorry." She headed toward the door.

"Carmen?"

She turned and looked at me.

"Kelly, the nurse, told me your name. I'm Hank."

She waited for me.

"I'm not very good with words. Not like my brother." I cleared my throat, and she walked toward me. "Words flowed from his mouth like music from an orchestra. But with me, words dribble out of my mouth like a kindergarten chorus."

She softly smiled. For all the height difference between us, her blue eyes never left mine. "But I'd like you to know that I very much appreciate what you did for my brother."

She kept looking at me, searching for something.

"I hope you don't blame yourself," I said.

Her head dropped, and she covered her face with her hands.

"Oh, hey, hey, hey. This wasn't your fault. You're a hero."

Her hands flew from her face. "If I was a hero, your brother would still be alive. I'm no hero. Loser, maybe, but not a hero."

"How are you a loser?"

"I literally lost Hunter. He lost his life in my hands. My efforts at CPR could not change the outcome, and it haunts me." Her voice was strong, but the hurt in her eyes shone stronger.

"It would haunt anyone, but that doesn't mean you're a loser. You did everything you could."

"I'm just afraid…."

"What?" I tried to get close to her without crowding or coming off as some creeper.

"When he opened the door to his hotel room, the look on his face was surprise, but also relief. I could tell he thought I was going to save him. But I didn't. What if his final thoughts were that I failed him?"

"My brother didn't think that way." I crouched to bridge the difference between my six-foot-six and her five-four-ish height and maintain eye contact when I spoke to her. "Hunter wasn't like that."

She had to weigh a buck twenty at best, but what she

lacked in size she made up for in personality. Her smile was gentle, and a dimple appeared on the side of her face. "You have his eyes," she said.

I grinned. "Well, actually he has mine. I was born first." Her face softened.

"And my mom would say we have our father's eyes."

At that comment, she glanced at the door. "Oh, your family. Are they here?"

"My mom and dad went back to their hotel."

"Are they staying at the Point?" She waved her hands as if to erase what she said. "I mean the Waterfront Point Resort."

I shook my head slightly. "No. Michael Harpington offered us rooms, but it was just too much for my folks. He put us up at Newport Heights."

She slowly nodded.

I stood to avoid the creep factor. "Thank you for coming."

"Of course." Her eyes widened. "Oh. I'm sorry. I'm taking time away from you and your brother."

"I've already said…." I pinched my eyes, but they still watered. I brushed my chin against the sleeve of my shirt and looked in my brother's direction. From this distance he looked like he was sleeping. "Somehow I had hoped that maybe when they discontinued life support he'd come out of it. You know?" I turned to Carmen, whose eyes were a salve.

"Yes. I do. This isn't how I wanted things to end."

"Me either. I was on the phone with him…."

"Oh." For a brief moment, her eyes registered the

connection. "I spoke to you."

I slowly nodded. "Yah, I heard everything. That's why I know how hard you tried to save my brother." I pushed my shoulders back like I was about to make a tackle, when really I just didn't want to lose my shit in front of this girl in light of what I wanted to say. "You didn't fail him." I cleared my throat. "Because of you, my brother didn't die alone."

###

His eyes may be the same mixture of green and brown as his brother's, but when he spoke they looked directly at me. It felt like he could see inside me—to my hurt, my pain, my fears.

"Do you mind if we step outside? I mean, unless you need more time with my brother. I understand, I just...." The sadness in his eyes finished the sentence for him.

"No, thank you. I'm finished."

Where Hunter was tall and lean, Hank was built like a pier pylon. Solid, round, and from the size of his arms he could hoist a ton of weight above him. He was stronger, sturdier, and towered over me. He held the door open for me, and I walked beneath the thick branch of his arm. He paused and looked back. "Uh, I just need a minute...."

"Sure." I turned to leave, and he gently caught my arm.

"Will you wait?"

I recognized the sound of someone who had waited while others grieved and now needed someone to stay with them while they grieved.

"I can wait outside or I can stay in the room—whatever is more comfortable." I couldn't tell if he was confused by what I said or comforted.

"Unless that would be too weird for you."

"Not weird at all."

I stepped back into his brother's hospital room, and when he walked toward Hunter, I stood respectfully to the side but within reach.

"Hey, little brother." His broad shoulders shook, and his rugged face crumpled with a pain I knew all too well. Losing someone that was so deeply etched in your heart felt like you'd never be right again. And in a way, you weren't. Going from having an incredible connection and love with someone to an unbelievable loss, was a pain rooted deep in your soul. The ache was constant.

"Man, I don't know what the hell you were doing eating those stupid chicken wings. It's only a thousand dollars." His head tilted toward the ceiling. "I would've given you the damn thousand to have you here." His hands looked like baseball mitts, gripping the side rail of the hospital bed that was still raised to protect Hunter from falling out, as if that were still possible. Hank's knuckles turned white, and I was sure he could lift the bed easily with one hand. He had the strength of ten men and the grief of a thousand.

"We had so many plans together. You and I were supposed to be each other's best man at our weddings and raise our kids together." His hands clenched the side rail tighter. "What the hell, Hunter? When I go on another failed blind date or eat so much pasta that I'm sick to my stomach, but still want dessert—who am I going to call? You were always my first call."

His loss was heartbreaking, and I ached in silence for this gentle giant.

"Who am I going to share these memories with? Hell, little brother, what memories will I have without you?"

I bit my lip to stop it from trembling. *I didn't do enough. Why couldn't I have saved him?*

"Dammit, Hunter."

I didn't have to know Hank long to know that he wasn't somebody that cursed, if you could even call dammit cursing. His large frame leaned over, and he gently brushed back his brother's hair and softly kissed his forehead.

The only sound I heard was the guttural cry of a wounded man who lost someone too early in life. He leaned on his brother and placed his head on his chest. I'd done the same thing with Mamá, hoping my love was enough to bring her back. Praying that I would feel her heartbeat and that the doctors had made a mistake, that she was simply resting. I'd imagined her hand gently on my head, stroking my hair, telling me how *bonita* I was. *Oh, Mamá, what should I do?*

Her absence from my life hadn't stopped me from turning to her and then listening. Sometimes she was loud and ever-present in my ear. Other times, like this evening, she was a faint whisper. *Consuelalo,* mija. Comfort him, my daughter. A calming presence came over me. I quietly approached Hank and placed my hand on his head. His hair was cut military style, but the buzzed edges were soft to the touch, and as I brushed the back of his head, his hair slipped between my fingers, until all I felt was him.

"You're not alone." The words came out of my mouth without conscious thought. Maybe it's what I'd needed to hear when Mamá died. Maybe he didn't need to hear it. Maybe I just needed to say it.

"I just want him back." Hank's voice was raw, and his eyes spilled tears.

I swallowed. There wasn't a day that went by that I didn't want to pick up the phone, hear her voice, and say, "*Hola, Madre.*"

I said the only other thing I knew to say. "I'm so sorry."

"Me too." Hank leaned his head against my hand. "Thank you."

"*De nada.*" I clenched my jaw. *English, Carmen,* Inglés. "I mean, it's nothing. No trouble."

He lifted his head off his brother and gently smiled. "I may know *muy poco Español*, but I got the gist."

I tilted my head. "Gracias."

He stood before his brother, placed his hand on his chest, and closed his eyes.

I bowed my head and silently prayed for a man I barely knew, and another man whose loss and grief I more than understood. Hank was like a brother in sorrow, but I was secretly glad we weren't related. Tragedy and destiny couldn't have brought us together for something as platonic as just friendship.

Hank walked with me to my car. "So, will you and your parents be heading back home?"

He tipped his head, the question on his face.

"When Katie and I checked your brother into his suite, uh… well, anyway, his zip code was listed and it was from Oregon, right?"

"Newport, Oregon. Nothing like Newport Beach, California, but I think it's better."

"My mamá used to say having pride in where you're from is important."

"I agree. So where are you from? What brings you pride?"

"I like to tell people that I was born in America, but I was conceived in May-he-co."

He gave me the look everyone did when I pronounced my country's name correctly.

"Letters are pronounced different in Spanish. *J* and *X* are pronounced like *H* and *E*. And *A* and *I* are pronounced like *E*. Basically the vowels *A-E-I-O-U* sound like Ah-A-E-O-Ew. The Me in Mexico is pronounced like 'may' because the *E* sounds like an *A*. The *X-I* sounds like 'he' because *X* is like *H*, and the vowel *I* is like *E*." I came up for air and saw I hadn't lost Hank's attention. If anything, he seemed genuinely interested; either that or my rant was the perfect distraction.

"Anyway, the 'co' in Mexico is the same in English and Spanish. In fact, *O* sounds the same in both languages. So oddly enough, I do know how to pronounce my own country's name in my own language. But to Americans, when I say Mexico, it sounds wrong."

His smile erased some of the sadness in his eyes. "I'm not sure what your job is at the hotel, but you should teach. That made perfect sense. I've heard Mexico pronounced like May-he-co, but until now I was too embarrassed to ask if I was saying it incorrectly or if they were."

I grinned. "It's a long answer to your question. But now you'll understand that I have pride for Mexico and Costa Mesa, California, where I was born and raised."

"I think we passed signs for Costa Mesa on the freeway when we drove from John Wayne Airport."

"You probably did. My girlfriend, Katie, calls me Carmen from Costa Mexico."

Hank's laughter was as husky as he was.

"Well, Carmen from Costa May-he-co, where can a big guy like me get something hearty to fill my stomach without emptying my bank account?"

"I know just the place."

CHAPTER **TEN**

"Am I dressed okay for this place?" I asked, looking at my jeans and black T-shirt. When I glanced up, Carmen was smiling. And when she smiled, it felt like the weight of the world lifted from my shoulders. For a moment, I didn't think of my brother. But as soon as I inhaled, the sharp pain in the pit of my gut pierced me. His loss was not something I'd get over. I'd feel it every time I breathed.

"Hey, you okay?"

Carmen was one of those people my dad called intuitive. She just got it. She had her finger on people's pulse, and it showed in the concern that reflected in her blue eyes. If you could call them blue. Her eyes reminded me of the Oregon Coast after a good rain, when the water was such an iridescent blue you could see the sand beneath your feet.

"Yah." I shrugged. "I'm okay. Just probably hungry."

"Well, where I'm taking you is one of those 'come as you are' places." She pointed toward a rust-colored truck, or maybe it was just rust. It was hard to tell the difference.

"You can follow me."

"Uh… actually, I don't have a car. My parents took the rental when they went back to the hotel."

Her eyes widened, and it felt like I could see all the way to the Oregon Coast. "Duh. I didn't even think of that. I'll drive, and after dinner I'll take you back to your hotel."

"You sure? That seems like a lot of driving."

When Carmen laughed it was as silky as her hair and had the same effect on me—I was mesmerized. Still, I wasn't sure why she laughed.

"What did I say that was so funny?"

"My job at the hotel is at the front drive. I drive all the time, but never far enough to enjoy it."

"You're a valet?"

She raised her eyebrows. "At your service." We stopped in front of the passenger-side door.

"Right on. That's badass."

"Gracias. It's how I met your brother…." She trailed off as she fumbled with the keys to unlock my door. I gently reached for her trembling hand.

"Carmen, it's okay. I'd like to know how you met Hunter. All I know is how hard you tried to save him."

When she tilted her head, the setting sun cast light on the ponytail that swung behind her. "You're very kind, Hank Hughes."

"Nah. I just know my brother, and I guarantee you if Hunter were in my spot, he'd do the same thing. He wouldn't want you to blame yourself. Neither do I. If Hunter were here, he'd want to know what you thought of me." I chuckled. "Although knowing Hunter, he wouldn't really care. He'd be more interested in making a play for you."

Her cheeks tinged with color. "He was a bit of a flirt."

"Oh, was he now?"

She held the door open for me. "Little bit."

I raised my eyebrow at her. "Now see, what'd I tell you? My brother never let a pretty girl pass without making sure she knew he was there." I shook my head and smiled, but then a feeling arose out of nowhere. *Why was a valet in my brother's hotel room?* "I hope my brother didn't say or do anything inappropriate." She held the door, and when I sat in her truck we were at eye level.

"Not at all. He was a perfect gentleman."

"Really? Is that why you went to his room?"

She broke eye contact with me. "No. I mean, it's complicated." She closed the door on me and the conversation. There was something Carmen wasn't telling me, and I wouldn't leave her or California until I knew.

CHAPTER **ELEVEN**

The easy energy between Hank and me shifted. I pulled into the driveway and nodded toward the front door.

"Welcome to *mi casa*." It was the most I'd said since he asked why I'd gone to his brother's room.

He stared out the side window. "Come as you are?"

"Exactly." I pulled the keys out of the ignition and twirled them around my finger. *Just tell him. So what if you embarrass yourself. It's worse if he doesn't know.* "Hank?"

He barely made eye contact with me, something I already knew was unusual for this man.

"The reason I went to your brother's room was to save my ass and to get a better look at his." The truth flowed out in one fluid sentence that probably could have benefited from some of Katie's wordsmithing and finessing, but hell, it was out there.

He slowly nodded and turned toward me. "Hunter did have a good ass."

I smiled, and felt the heat rush from my throat to my face.

"I got so flustered when I met your brother that I forgot to get his last name. And without his last name, I couldn't—"

"Charge his parking to his room."

"Exactly." *How does he know hotel protocol?* I looked at him and he smiled. "Anyway"—I shook my head— "my friend, Katie, helped. Her computer is loaded with the new software, FrogKiss, which," I held up my hand and the keys settled in my palm, "I only recently found out, from a quick glance at your brother's hotel profile, that he was the creator."

The green and brown in his eyes blended together, and for a moment I saw his brother.

"So, we were searching the software for Hunter's hotel room to charge his car when my boss showed up. And to cover my ass because I wasn't at the front drive, Katie said that your brother changed rooms. Of course, he hadn't, which is why we went to see him. We were going to ask if he'd mind swapping rooms."

"Why didn't you just tell me that?"

I wanted to look anywhere but at him, but the honesty in Hank's face made it impossible to turn away.

"I was embarrassed and...." Sadness returned. "I felt like because I lied that maybe it had something to do with what happened to your brother."

His laughter startled me. "Karma doesn't work that way. Hunter put too many chicken wings in his mouth because he's always wanted to win this stupid chicken-eating contest in our hometown."

"Thanks, but it's not karma. It's Catholic guilt, which I

think is worse. Catholic guilt is the gift that keeps on giving and one that you can never seem to return."

He smiled slightly. "I'm not Catholic, but I understand guilt."

"What do you have to feel guilty about?" My question was probably too personal, but if we were baring souls, we were baring everything.

"Hell, where do I begin?" He rubbed his face with his hand, but it didn't erase the regret that clung to him like a dark shadow he couldn't outrun. "Well, for starters, I was supposed to go with Hunter on this trip. We planned it for weeks, but then…."

"What?"

"I let work get in the way."

"I'm sure he understood."

"Oh, yah, Hunter was great. Said I'd be the one missing out on all the California girls he'd see from his beachfront hotel." He smiled. "But then… when I was on the phone with him, I knew something was wrong. But I didn't get off the phone. I should have called 911, but I…."

"Froze?"

"Yah, I froze." Defeat filled the space between us.

"Hank, so did I. I totally froze. I couldn't remember how to perform CPR, and we're trained on it, like, every other month. But in the moment, it was crazy. Everything I knew vanished from my head like it had never been there. I barely knew your brother, and I was a mess. I can't *even* imagine what it was like for you."

Relief washed over his face.

"This was your brother," I said. "If I had been in your place, I wouldn't have done anything differently. I would have stayed on the phone. I wouldn't have wanted to leave him." My eyes stung with tears.

The rugged features of his face softened. "I didn't want to leave him either—on the phone or at the hospital." He brushed the top of his head and his short, spiky hair moved back and forth. "If you weren't at the hospital, I think I'd still be with him."

"I know how that feels." A tear slipped down my cheek, and I brushed it away. "Three years ago, my mamá died, and I was the last one to leave."

"Oh." His brow lost the tension that furrowed it. "I'm sorry."

I raised my shoulders. "I didn't know how to leave. For months I went to the hospital every day to be with her. I was so solidly in this mode of taking care of her that I didn't think about anything else. I was on autopilot. Even when she began to lose her memory from all the drugs, I went. One time an orderly asked me, 'Why do you go visit her so much? She doesn't know you.' And I said, 'That doesn't matter. I know her.'" I lowered my head and felt the memory stream down my face.

"Carmen." Hank moved across the seat toward me and pulled me into his arms. This man I didn't even know, knew what I needed. His embrace was all-encompassing, and in his arms I felt guarded from sorrow.

"When I took care of my mamá, there was this sense of control over the circumstances. Yet in the end, she took that all away from me when she chose to stop treatment. I was so hurt, because she had already given up when I was still fighting really hard for her."

"As crazy as this sounds, I was mad at Hunter for not fighting harder. But a life on a ventilator is no life."

I looked into his eyes. "I know it's no life, but I still wanted her here."

His lips were close enough to touch, but it was his eyes that connected with me. They saw through me. "That's not how you would want to have her. Any more than it's how I would want Hunter."

I wasn't expecting Hank when I went to the hospital, this mammoth man whose heart beat rapidly against mine.

"Hungry?" he asked.

I smiled. "Yes, and I'm sure my entire family has been watching from the front window."

He grinned. "Then let's go give them the real thing."

CHAPTER **TWELVE**

"So your name is Huge?"

"*Ay caramba,* Julia! His name is Hank. His last name is Hughes."

"Huge?" Julia asked as she placed the baking dish of enchiladas in the center of the kitchen table.

"Are you deaf?" I asked.

"Hughes," Hank said above our raised voices. "Nowhere as rich as Howard Hughes, but we're not batshit crazy either."

"Oh sure, Howard Hughes, the aviator," Tomás said. "Good movie with Leonardo DiCaprio."

I slapped my forehead. "You're all *locos.*"

Julia looked at me and playfully raised the spatula in her hand like she was going to smack me with it, but if it'd stop her questions, then she could beat me like a piñata.

"Well," she said with a subtle edge to her voice, "Hughes is like huge, and Hank is large and as solid as a tank."

"One of my buddies in Newport calls me 'Hank the

Tank,'" he said, as if my cousin's comment was nothing short of a compliment.

"You're not offended?" I said.

Hank's hearty laughter even made my papá, who sat quietly at the end of the table, smile. "I am built like a tank, and my brother Hunter is… was." He cleared his throat. "Well, Hunter was a giant in his field. Anyway, together we were the brains and brawn."

"I was sorry to hear of your loss," my papá said.

"Thank you, sir."

"He choked, is that correct?" Papá asked. But somehow his question didn't seem intrusive.

Hank slowly nodded. "My little brother had all the book smarts a person could have, he was brilliant. But…." He paused. "He lacked street smarts. Hunter always told me that street smarts trumped book smarts any day. And I guess I wish it had been a lack of street smarts that caused his death, but it was something as simple as common sense."

"The two, though, are very intricately woven," Papá said.

Hank stared at the end of the table, considering the words. "Yes, sir, I think they are."

"My Carmen is very street savvy, probably too much for her own good, which is why I made sure she used some of her mamá's money to go back to school."

I shook my head. "Papá, I didn't use any of Mamá's money. What the hotel doesn't pay in tuition, I do with what I make at the hotel."

"That's got to be tough," Hank said. "Balancing work

and college."

With all eyes on me, I tipped my chin as if I were braver than I felt. "It's no big deal. I can handle it."

Hank grinned. "I don't doubt you can. What are you studying?"

"Computer programming."

His grin spread into a full smile. "No wonder you and Hunter hit it off so well."

"I didn't know what he did until after—"

"Mija," my abuelita's voice came to the rescue. She walked from the kitchen into the dining room. "Why don't you say grace so we can begin?"

Hank lowered his head, and I reached for his hand. "We hold hands."

"Hell, I'd hold my breath for a minute and a half while you say grace if it meant we could start eating in just ninety seconds. But," he looked at me and squeezed my hand, "if you're still praying after that, I'll be inhaling oxygen and enchiladas at the ninety-first second, and not necessarily in that order."

Laughter filled the room.

"Bless us, O Lord, and these thy gifts, which we are about to receive from thy bounty, through Christ our Lord. Amen."

"Amen!" Hank gave one last tug on my hand before releasing it under the table. He glanced at Julia, then my father, but it was my abuelita who picked up his plate and loaded it with homemade beans and rice, and topped four enchiladas with mole sauce.

"Now don't be frightened because it's green," Abuelita said. "These are *enchiladas de pollo con salsa verde*, or chicken enchiladas with green salsa. The green comes from the tomatillos."

"I'm from Oregon, ma'am, where it's greener than St. Patrick's Day, so that enchilada sauce is right up my alley," Hank said, and appeared to be waiting until everyone had food on their plate.

"Begin, begin!" Papá said, with his wine glass raised toward Hank.

Hank lifted his fork in return. "And may it never end."

CHAPTER THIRTEEN

The Newport Heights hotel was in the heart of the coastal community of Newport and overlooked the Pacific Ocean. I sat in Carmen's truck and nodded toward the bellman, who reluctantly began his approach toward us.

"He doesn't look too happy," she said.

I shrugged. "Screw him. If he judges a person by what they drive, then he's not worth much." I glanced at her just to see if she was smiling, which she was.

"Sometimes the people that drive the shittiest cars are the ones that leave the best tips."

I laughed. "I bet."

"It's true. It's like they're apologizing for their car."

"Either that or they're loaded and just don't want to draw attention to it. Anyone who stays at the Waterfront Point Resort can't be cheap. The rooms cost a king's ransom."

"Not any more than the Heights. There aren't any bad rooms, either," she said. "Or at least that's what I'm told."

"I don't know what the big deal is. All the rooms have

a step-out balcony with a view of the ocean. My parents have a furnished patio that looks toward the harbor, but it's nothing we don't offer in Oregon. Except in Newport, Oregon, we don't have a snobbery surcharge and elitism excise."

"I get the snobbery part, but what's an excise?"

"It's a tax on certain goods and services hotels charge, for things like cigarettes and alcohol," I said from rote memory.

"What exactly *do* you do in Oregon?"

The valet reached for my door handle. I quickly turned to Carmen. "Did you have any plans? I mean after you dropped me off?"

"I was going to go to church," she said.

"Oh, I don't go to church."

She opened her door, left her keys in the ignition, and smiled. "Neither do I."

Confidence in a woman was sexy as hell, and Carmen exuded it. She tipped her chin toward the valet. "Keys are inside. Don't scratch her."

The valet took one look at the rust bucket and his only response was to ask, "Will you be checking any bags this evening?"

"The night's still young." She turned to me and raised an eyebrow. "I'm not sure."

I shook my head. "You're trouble."

"Perhaps." She brushed past me and walked into the foyer of the hotel as if she knew its layout, which I wasn't sure she didn't.

When we passed the fine-dining restaurant, she turned

down a back hallway. In the distance, a red exit light glowed from the ceiling. She glanced over her shoulder.

"You haven't lost me yet," I said.

Her ponytail swung behind her. "Vamonos!"

"You're a bossy little thing, aren't ya?" I briskly walked past her to reach the door before she did. "This isn't going to set off an alarm, is it?"

She shrugged. "No lo sé."

"English, *por favor*?"

"I don't know." She giggled, and the hard edge she so fiercely maintained fell from her shoulders like Atlas had finally been relieved of his burden.

"That's better," I said with a nod, and pushed against the stainless steel bar that stretched across the back of the door. The door opened to the echo of waves striking the beach.

"Welcome to church." Carmen kicked off her flip-flops and pulled her hair out of its ponytail. It was longer than I'd imagined, with a sheen to it that made me want to touch it just to see what it felt like.

She looked at me. I quickly followed suit, stuffing my socks into my shoes and stashing them behind the door. I rolled the cuffs of my jeans and saw Carmen doing the same thing.

"Anywhere from Canada to Cape Horn, my church is any beach lining the Pacific Ocean," Carmen said.

A half-moon shone enough light for us to find our way to the water's edge.

"It's impossible not to believe in something bigger than myself when there's an endless ocean before me and a starry sky above me," she said.

The tide lapped our feet and tickled my toes. "What do you do when you come out here?"

Carmen dug her feet in the sand, and air bubbles popped across the wet mounds. "That's the beauty, I don't have to *do* anything. I get to just be. Nothing's expected of me here."

"It's not like any church I've been to."

"Church is a building where people meet. This is spiritual. This is where I go to meet God."

I stood beside her and watched the waves rise and fall. God was not a topic I wanted to discuss. Hunter was gone, and it felt like any higher anything was gone, too.

"Sometimes when I've been writing code all day, I come here to free all those crazy thoughts that buzz around me."

"Does it work?"

"Hasn't let me down yet."

"It's funny, I live by the beach and my job is located on beachfront property, but it's almost as if I forget it's there until I travel hundreds of miles, and suddenly it's like I'm seeing the ocean for the first time. Weird, right?"

"Nah, that's what my mamá called refrigerator blindness. We never see what's right in front of us. In fact, I only started coming here religiously after she died."

"My buddy Oliver did the same thing after his mom died."

"It's probably Mother Nature's way of returning us to Mother Earth."

A wave crested, and for a moment the white tops froze before it slammed against the ocean floor.

"There is something about its magnitude that makes me feel small."

Carmen laughed. "I can't imagine anything making you feel small, but the Pacific certainly has the best shot."

The tide inched forward as the waves crashed closer to shore.

"So, what happens now?" It was the first time she turned her attention away from church to me.

What, now that I've met you and I'd like to know more? We may live on the same coast, but there's a thousand miles of beach between us.

"Will you and your parents bring Hunter back to Oregon?"

Hunter. I stared toward the ocean that seemed as bottomless as the pit in my stomach that no amount of homemade Mexican food could fill. Or Carmen. I watched the cadence of waves hit the shore. The repetitive nature of its never-ending cycle was oddly reassuring. She was right. The ocean didn't want or expect anything from me.

"This is probably not what you want to talk about," she said, filling the silence.

"He's going to be cremated, and later we'll spread his ashes in Oregon. I don't think my mom's ready to let go."

"I'm so sorry."

Three little words people said so frequently, they almost lost meaning.

"The sun will rise tomorrow." I finally looked at her. If it were at all possible, the moonlight only made her more beautiful. *Why now? Why do I meet someone like her now?*

"The sun will rise tomorrow?"

"It's something my football coach would say when we were too stressed out, lost a game, or made a mistake. In the worst situations he'd say, 'Boys, the sun will rise tomorrow' to remind us that whatever happened, it would feel differently tomorrow. It may not go away, but it wouldn't sting as much."

The edge of the clouds had a purple hue that reminded me of my brother. "When Hunter was in the eighth grade, I was a sophomore in high school."

I picked up a piece of driftwood and threw it in the ocean like a shot put. "Anyway, one Friday night Hunter and I snuck out of our house, and my buddy Jacob, who had taken his parents' car, picked up the gang."

"The gang?"

"My buddies. There was Oliver, his twin brother, Reid, Bryan, Jacob, Hunter, and me. We took turns driving from Newport to Portland to see Prince in concert."

"Did your parents ever find out?" The curiosity in her voice made me smile.

"It was never confirmed, but they had their suspicions. We probably would have gotten away with it if Hunter hadn't decided after the concert that all he wanted to wear was purple. My mom knew something was up." I shook my head. "That kid was so damn goofy. He wore purple shirts, shorts, hell, my mom even found a pair of purple Converse. His entire eighth grade year he wore purple, and I think that's when my folks figured out that we may have gone to Portland to see Prince in concert."

"Is it a far drive to Portland?"

"Driving from Newport to Portland is like driving from your house in Costa Mexico to San Diego. It's a long drive, and from what I saw on GPS, the terrain is similar. There're a lot of spots between Newport and Portland that don't have much, so if you break down you're SOL."

"I never would have taken you for a renegade. You seem like a by-the-book kind of guy."

"Then you don't know me." My tone was curt. *Well, that was a dick move.*

"You're right," she said, and crossed her arms over her chest. "I don't."

"Fair enough." Keeping her at a distance wouldn't make leaving any easier, but still, it felt like the one thing I could control. But I didn't have to be a dick, so I softened my edge. "Most people think Hunter was the reckless one, but I did my fair share to add to my parents' gray hair."

Carmen giggled. "Papá says I'm the reason for all his gray hair."

"He seems like a good guy. Do you all live together?"

"Nah. Papá lives in Costa Mesa, but not with my cousin. He couldn't stay in the home he shared with Mamá, so he sold their house and bought a condo."

"That must have been hard."

Her hair brushed across her shoulders. "Not really. My cousin needed help paying the mortgage and had a guest room that was rarely used, so I offered to rent the room, and it all worked out." She studied me with eyes that pierced through me. "I never imagined anything working out after

Mamá died, but it did.”

I slowly nodded. *She's trying to connect. Stop being a douche and go with the moment. What the hell is wrong with you?*

“Do you live with your parents?” she asked.

I assumed it was a joke, or maybe my mood had turned as dark as the water, but when I saw the inquisitive look on her face, I realized it wasn't.

“No, after college I borrowed some money from my folks to put down on a condo. Hunter crashed with me when he wasn't off installing some new program.” I paused. “But my folks have an apartment unit above their garage that I may temporarily move into when I return to Oregon.” I laughed. “It'll save on gas, because I know I'll be checking on my folks every day. Better to just stay close by for a while, you know, until everything….”

“Of course.” She slowly nodded. “So, Hunter stayed with you when he wasn't installing new programs. Is that what he was doing at the Waterfront?”

Why is she so interested? What the hell does it matter now what Hunter was doing?

“Was he installing new software?”

She is employed by Michael Harpington. From what Hunter told me, the guy would make the most trusting and naïve person incredibly suspicious. *I may not be as bright as my brother, but I'm nobody's fool.* I didn't really know Carmen to know how much to reveal. What my brother did was his business, and not mine to share. Not until I knew more.

"I thought maybe he was just checking on FrogKiss," she said.

I grabbed another piece of wood and flung it into the ocean. "Something like that."

CHAPTER **FOURTEEN**

"So, he just left?" Katie's brown eyes reflected the emotion I felt—confusion.

"One minute we were on the beach, and then it's like he suddenly learned Spanish and told me, 'Adios, amiga,' because I haven't seen or heard from him since."

Katie laughed. "Maybe he had to go to the bathroom or something."

"And never came back?"

She pursed her lips together in thought.

"Not likely," I said. "We walked back from the beach to the hotel together, and when I turned around he had gone one way and so… I went the other." My stomach churned, remembering how hollow it felt to see him by the elevators without as much as a goodbye.

"Did you do something? Or maybe say something?"

If frustrated had a look, I wore it. "No, I didn't *do* anything."

"Carm, why would he just leave? I mean, from what you

told me you two really connected. Granted, it had to be the *worst* situation imaginable," empathy filled the small space in her office, "but in that tragedy, you made a connection." She paused and leaned back in her chair. "Or…."

"Or what?" I crossed my arms over my chest.

"Don't take that defensive stance with me, missy."

I rolled my eyes. "You're not in Human Resources anymore. My stance isn't defensive." I uncrossed my arms and flung them out. "It's taking *offense* to this conversation."

"Who's offended?"

I rubbed my forehead, but the headache was eminent. "Por qué yo?"

"Why you?" Bogart elbowed me. "Why you, what?"

I glanced at Katie's husband. "Why is my life in the middle of yours? I just came in hoping for an answer."

"What's your question?" Bogart leaned his palm on the side of his tool belt and took a broad stance in Katie's office. If his stance said anything, it would be either, "Look at me, I'm the sheriff of Tool Town" or "Does anyone know where the Village People convention is?" The guy was one of my closest friends, but sometimes he was goofy as hell.

"Carmen met Hank at the hospital," Katie said. "He's the brother of Hunter, the guy…."

"I remember." Bogart's face softened when he looked at his wife. The love he showed in that one glance was what fairy tales were made of, and reminded me of Hank's green-brown eyes when he looked at me. I shook my head. *Stop reading into things. Hank was just being nice. He has kind eyes, that's all.*

Bogart turned to me. "So, you met Hank, and what?"

"They were hitting it off, but then he just left," Katie said.

Bogart waggled his eyebrows. It must be a trait he inherited in his marriage. "Hitting it off, huh? How hard did you hit it?"

I squared him off with a hard stare. "Yeah, because that's so like me, isn't it?"

He grinned. "Oh, all right. So, your question is what? Why he left?"

"Si."

Bogart rubbed the dark stubble on his chin. "Well, I don't know the guy, but he just lost his brother, so he's probably not thinking too straight right now."

I slowly nodded.

"Did you kiss?" The tone of his voice was serious, not sarcastic.

I shook my head.

"But you would have liked to," he stated, rather than asked.

It felt like my stomach had been turned inside out. "*Si*. Is that crazy? I barely know him."

"Not at all." Bogart elbowed me and then offered an encouraging smile. "Then go see him."

"And say what?" Katie asked the question before I could. "He lives in Oregon."

"Katie's right. It'll never work. I barely know the guy, and long-distance relationships are short-term for a reason."

"Who's talking about a relationship?" Bogart came back

at me. "I'm just saying to go see the guy."

"Maybe."

"What else do you have to do?" Bogart said.

"Oh, I don't know, pick up my uniform from Housekeeping and work my shift at the front drive?"

"I misspoke," Bogart said. "What I meant to say is go see the guy before he leaves. If nothing else, tell him goodbye. Then you'll have peace with it either way."

I must not have seemed convinced, because Bogart got right up in my face.

"Carmen, what do you have to lose?" But he didn't allow me to answer. "If you go to him and he's still standoffish, at least you'll know you tried, and we'll be here to support you because, hey, we're hotel family and that's what families do. But if you do absolutely nothing and let him go without seeing him, then we'll forever mock you and throw this cowardly failure right back in your face, because, hey, we're family and that's what hotel families do."

"I'm not being cowardly."

"That's all you got from what he said?" Katie said, rolling her eyes. "Do you even hear yourself? Carm, you like this guy. And that's okay." Her brown eyes softened along with her voice. "You're the one who reminded me that when you're attracted to someone despite the circumstances, that doesn't make it wrong. It just makes it real, and I think real scares you."

"I'm not scared, and I'm not cowardly." I was about to cross my arms over my chest, but that would completely disprove my point.

"Good." Bogart smiled. "Then when your shift ends, the Newport Heights is on your way home. Drop in and say your piece."

I glanced at Katie, and then back to Bogart. "I barely know him. And what I felt was probably nothing more than all those emotions from saying goodbye to his brother. This is stupid."

"Carm." Katie's voice was soothing. "You're just going for clarification and to know where you stand, because maybe he felt the same thing. And maybe it freaked him out too."

"Maybe," I said.

"Keep your cool and your dignity intact," she said.

This made me smile. Katie knew me well.

"But," she said seriously, "if this Hank guy decides to take the low road, then just kick him to the curb, and I'll be there to run over the bastard, because as my husband said, we're family."

CHAPTER **FIFTEEN**

The hallway that led from Katie's office to Housekeeping began at ground level and descended the closer I got to the laundry room. Unlike the hospital, the hallway was void of framed artwork. Instead, the employee of the month plaques and their pictures hung in the back Housekeeping hallway, because nothing said job well done like a police-quality mug shot buried in the basement.

They blurred past me, along with my conversation with Katie and Bogart. *If I had some reason to see Hank, that'd be one thing, but to just show up and ask what happened? Awkward.* Nope. It's like Bogart said, he'd just lost his brother, and we barely knew each other. If my feelings were butt-hurt, it was a small price to pay for not being able to save Hunter.

The pungent, acrid thickness from the dry cleaning solvents never failed to make my eyes water. A pop followed by a swoosh when the hydraulic press was released caused a billow of steam that seemed to vaporize just as quickly as it surfaced.

Pablo. Undoubtedly he was at the helm. His rhythm with the steam press was nothing short of seamless. No one in Housekeeping turned around the guest and staff laundry faster than Pablo. And when he put a crease in my black uniform slacks, it made the plain pants look stylish, sophisticated, and as sharp as the vertical pleat running down the front.

When Richard chose to add a bow tie and white bibbed shirt to the front drive uniforms, we went from looking like valets to maître d's or Vegas blackjack dealers. Pablo was the only highlight to our new uniform standard.

"Hey." I approached the counter that separated me from him.

"Hey yourself." He wiped the beads of sweat from his forehead. "Remember how I'm always telling you to check your pockets?"

"And remember how I said that if I left anything in my pocket, it was your tip?"

When he shook his head, his thick hair that had silvered beautifully swooped over his ears. Combined with black-framed glasses and skin that looked like the sun god kissed it herself, Pablo had the hot Latino guy from the telenovelas thing going on that was simply *muy bueno*. The men on the Latino soaps, which my abuelita watched as religiously as she went to Mass, were equal parts super gentlemanly and respectful of the family, to manly men with horse ranches who'd fight for your love. Pablo was way too old for me, but that hadn't stopped me from imagining a season of something with him, which was how long telenovelas lasted. But the more I thought of Pablo, the more my thoughts turned to Hank. Hank could definitely last a season or two without breaking a sweat. *Me-wow*.

"It's a good thing I check pockets," Pablo said.

"Qué? Did I leave you a good tip?"

"No… or maybe… I don't know."

The mysteriousness of it all intrigued me, which reminded me again of Hank and how he'd just vanished. *What'd he do? Where'd he go? Was he meeting someone?* The only thing that was clear was that I watched way too many Latino soaps with my abuelita.

"What I'd leave?"

His glasses slid down the bridge of his nose and his dark eyes steadied on someone in the distance. He pulled the press down hard and steam frosted his lenses. I knew from the sudden move it was time to *callarse*. I zipped my lips and waited.

"Pablo, do you have the uniforms for the new valet?"

Jefe.

I turned with a forced grin. "Buenos días, Richard."

He grimaced as if I had just dropped an F-bomb, not wished the boss a good morning.

"Gonzalez," he grumbled, and returned his focus to Pablo. "I hope the uniforms are ready, because Bryce starts his shift today."

"Oh! Am I training someone?" I quickly tempered my enthusiasm. If Richard thought I was remotely interested, he'd reassign the job. "The occupancy rate is at ninety." I crossed my arms over my chest for good measure. Training pay was double, and I was one of the few valets who had completed the hotel's training program.

Richard squinted in my direction. "That was the general idea. And I'm well aware of the occupancy rate, Gonzalez."

My stomach jumped. *Double time. Ah, yah*!

"But you won't be training anyone if I don't have a uniform." His glance at Pablo was met with a hardened stare.

"Josie delivered the new uniform to the men's locker room," Pablo said.

"The men's locker room?" Richard's tone was as harsh as a slap. He gripped the counter that separated him from Pablo. "The dry cleaning slip was very specific, stating that I'd pick up the uniform to present to Bryce. He's the nephew of Mr. Harpington. The handling of his uniform was, as you'd say, *muy importante*. But apparently you only *speak* English."

"Actually, I speak, read, and write English, Spanish, and French perfectly well. My English was good enough for the owner, who specifically told me what to do. So, should I speak or write to Mr. Harpington in English, Spanish, or French about how you disapprove of his direct orders to me? Unless you care to address this issue with him directly, because I'm sure his door is always open to those who want to second-guess him."

Richard's face turned as red as the iron that Pablo used for linens.

"Your dry cleaning ticket was intercepted by Mr.

Harpington, who told me to have his nephew's uniform placed in the men's locker room just like everyone else's. He didn't want his nephew afforded any special treatment." Pablo slipped a dress shirt onto a wire hanger. "If you are unhappy with how I processed the order, you are more than welcome to take it up with Mr. Harpington or Human Resources, who I'm sure would be interested in how you treat the line staff." Pablo buttoned the collar on the starched shirt and hung it on the rod beside the other pristinely pressed garments.

"There'd be no reason to consult Human Resources if you'd just told me Mr. Harpington's request. Communication doesn't have to be this difficult, Pablo. I hope you'll remember this in the future." Richard pivoted away from the counter, and as he brushed past me his voice was as nasty as his breath. "Don't be late, Gonzalez."

"Si."

I waited until Dick was no longer visible in the hallway before I spoke. "Are you going to report him to Human Resources?"

When Pablo smiled, it reminded me of Hank. They both had a gentle, easygoing nature. "Now, Carmen, why would I do that and lose the edge I have with Richard? Do you really think he's ever going to talk to me like that again?"

"Yes. Yes, I do. The guy's a *pinche cabrón*."

"Every job has an asshole. It's about identifying who it is and then making sure you have them by the short hairs. And right now, I have Richard by the *cojones*."

I laughed. "You really think you have him by the balls?"

"Carmen, Carmen, Carmen." Pablo pulled the lever to lower the press onto a pair of black slacks. "As soon as I mentioned Human Resources, his tone may not have changed, but the look on his face did. He was scared. He's a manager. I'm a line employee. There's a great divide, and he's expected to be the leader in this situation, right?"

"Si."

"When you're confronted with a senior hotel member who's trying to exert their authority, remember that your power is in your position."

"Because they're supposed to be the leader?"

"Si. And you're a trainer, don't you remember the inverted pyramid?"

My brain felt as clouded as the steamed air between us.

Pablo pulled the slacks from the press and placed them on a hanger. He walked to the counter, grabbed the white tailor's chalk, and sketched an upside-down pyramid on a green apron.

"In a regular organizational chart, the top tier is top management and the tiers beneath that are middle management, supervisors, and the bottom rung of the pyramid, the widest one, is the line employees, right?"

I nodded, remembering the PowerPoint presentation that Janet in Human Resources droned on about during the training program. It was the only time the room was dark, and if her voice hadn't been so annoying, I would have fallen asleep. As it was, Pablo's picture refreshed my memory.

"But at the Waterfront Point," Pablo made air quotes, "'we do things differently.'" He sounded like one of the commercials the hotel had invested in after our staged walkout. "The pyramid is inverted so that top management is supposedly there to support the middle managers, supervisors and us lowly line employees. Each tier is there to support the other."

"Yeah, so? That all changed after we walked out for equal treatment."

"Exactly. Mr. Adams almost lost his job as General Manager, so he made it his mission to ensure the line staff was properly treated. How Richard just behaved, dumped the pyramid right back on its face."

"So, if he were reported, he'd be…."

"Adiós."

"Would that be so bad?" I asked.

"Carmen, better the devil you know than the devil you don't. And since you'll be training the owner's nephew today, we don't know what kind of devil he is or isn't." He wiped the pyramid away with the brush of his hand. "So be careful."

"I'm always careful."

Pablo wagged his finger as if I had taken a bite of dinner before saying grace.

"Qué?"

He reached beneath the counter and held a thumb drive between his index finger and thumb. "Mr. Harpington didn't just come down to talk to me about his nephew's uniform. That was simply the opener. He really wanted to know if I had come across any flash drive, hard drive, or computer disk that may have been bundled with the sheets and comforter from that young kid that died in room 1225."

"Hunter." His gentle face flashed across my mind. "His name was Hunter Hughes. And that flash drive was on his neck when I performed…." I glanced at the row of neatly pressed clothes behind Pablo. *What I wouldn't give for my emotions to be ironed out as smoothly.* Instead, I felt emotionally as unkempt as the pile of laundry waiting for Pablo's press.

"Carmen, everyone knows how hard you tried to save him."

"It wasn't enough. But this is." I reached for the thumb drive, but Pablo pulled his hand away.

"Not so quick, *señorita*. Whatever is on this is, as Richard said, *muy importante*."

"We don't know if it's important. Mr. Harpington may have just been collecting his belongings for his family, who are in town." My stomach turned a somersault. "Oh my gosh. Hank."

"Hank?"

"Hunter's brother. I can bring this to him." But Pablo wouldn't release it to me.

"Why would Mr. Harpington be so interested in this if it wasn't important?"

"Pablo, you've been around too many chemicals. It's just a flash drive."

He slowly shook his head. "I don't think so, *amiga*. If that was the case, then why didn't Mr. Harpington send someone else to ask about it? No. Whatever is on here is big enough to get Mr. Harpington off his ass."

I giggled.

"And maybe you can figure out what's on this before you give it to this Hank person," Pablo said.

"No. If I've learned anything in my college classes, it's that plugging an unknown flash drive into your laptop is akin to taking candy from a stranger. You have no idea what's inside." I stood back from the counter and distanced myself from Pablo. His good looks weren't enough to keep me away from Hank. And that flash drive was what I needed to go see him again.

"Besides," I said, "if there is something important stored on this, then Hunter probably encrypted it, and I don't have decryption software on my PC to access the data."

"Yes, but your college does."

"They probably do."

"Probably, Carmen?"

"Okay, they do. But why is this so important to you? You didn't even know Hunter."

"No, but I know Mr. Harpington, and I don't trust him. He came down here looking for this." He held the flash drive toward me. "And I think there's more on this than just personal files."

"Maybe there is, but it's none of our business."

"Carmen, what harm is there in taking this to a computer on your college campus and seeing what's on it?"

"Harm? Oh, I don't know. I really don't want to be known as 'Carmen the Grim Reaper of Electronics' who killed an entire college computer network with a virus-ridden thumb drive."

Pablo seemed to understand my concern, which lessened my defensiveness.

"What I *can* do is first find someone I trust in IT at the hotel to run a virus test. If the thumb drive is clean, then I'll go to campus and learn what's on it and go from there."

"Gracias."

"De nada," was my immediate response, when I wasn't sure why I was welcoming the opportunity to run blindly across a minefield and hope it didn't all blow up in my face.

CHAPTER **SIXTEEN**

"Hank, didn't I tell you that you should've minored in psychology?" Jacob said, looking into the camera to comb his hair with his fingers.

"I don't know what that has to do with losing Hunter." Oliver's blond hair and blue eyes popped into the Skype screen. "Hey, Hank!"

Jacob shoved him out of the frame so that he could finish arranging his hair. His mug filled the screen of my laptop.

"Psychology has nothing to do with what happened to Hunter." Jacob stopped perfecting his looks, if that were at all possible. He and Hunter vied—*had* vied—for best-looking in our group. Now Jacob alone held that title.

Hunter. My brother always Skyped when he was away on business. It was weird that he hadn't Skyped from his hotel room.

"I still can't believe he's gone," Jacob said.

I nodded.

"Me neither." Reid stood behind Jacob. If I didn't know

how to tell Oliver and Reid apart, I'd think it was Ollie again. But Reid's eyes were a darker shade of blue than his twin brother's.

"Hank, I'm so sorry." Bryan was beside Reid. Bryan's sunburnt face filled the screen. His work on the loading dock hauling inventory kept him in the sun. On the days I worked at the hotel, I joined Bryan whenever I could with whatever reason I could find to get out of the gloomy, dark purchasing department. Bryan was sunburnt year-round, and seeing his reddened cheeks was more fulfilling than the five-star room service that brought a bagel and cream cheese and cost thirty bucks.

"Listen, guys, Hank didn't call for us to bring him down. If you half-wits listened, his concern isn't about getting his brother back to Oregon. It's about wrapping up what Hunter was working on in Huntington Beach." Jacob continued to assume the lead. "And this little Carmen gal seems just as interested in Hunter's biz as Hank, which leads me back to psychology."

"Jacob, I've got to side with the guys. I'm still not sure what psychology has to do with Carmen," I said.

"Psychology is about understanding women," Jacob said without a hint of a smile.

"Uh, Jacob, as Sigmund Freud would say, 'In your dreams!'" Ollie laughed.

"No, brother," Reid said, elbowing his twin. "I think perhaps Oscar Wilde said it best: 'Women are meant to be loved, not to be understood.'"

"Yuck it up, guys." Jacob shooed them away like flies.

"But who's the one who always has a date and," he held his index finger toward the screen, "not just a date, but the hottest woman in the room?"

"He does always seem to get the cute girls." Bryan's burnt eyebrows raised. "True story."

"That's because I majored in business and earned my minor in psych. When it comes to women, I need all the help I can get, and I got that help in psych. And before you idiots ask, I don't consider it insider trading if my psych classes get me inside a girl's place for the night. I say all's fair, including using my psych classes to understand them better—and to better my odds of bedding them," Jacob said.

"You're serious," Reid said.

"Unbelievable," Ollie said.

"So how does that help Hank with this Carmen girl?" Bryan asked, then glanced at the computer camera and smiled. "Hey, Hank, she seems like a sweet girl."

"Thanks, buddy," I said.

"Well, for starters stop ditching her." Jacob shook his finger at the computer screen. "Next time you're with her, use the time to get to know what she knew. She was honest about why she went to see Hunter, to save her ass, and he had sparked her interest, so I don't think she'd lie to you. Not if she already told you that. You said she was in college working on a computer programming degree, right?"

I nodded.

"Then she's the perfect person. She speaks computer geek, which only Hunter did. Don't you have to go to the Waterfront Point to collect, uh, his belongings?" Jacob said.

"Yah. My parents asked if I wouldn't mind going for them."

"That's great," Jacob said. "I mean, it sucks, but the upside is that Carmen works at the front drive, right?"

"Yeah. If she's on duty."

"If she's not on duty, you already know where she lives. And if she is on duty, as she's parking your car, apologize," Jacob said.

"Apologize?" Ollie and Reid pulled a twin thing and spoke in tandem.

"What does Hank have to apologize for?" Bryan asked.

All their faces squeezed into the frame of my computer, each vying for more space. Their fighting was oddly comforting.

"Hank," Jacob said.

"I'm listening." I stopped staring at the keyboard and focused on my friend's face, which was sincere and truly trying to help as only Jacob knew how.

"Trust me, you get more flies with honey, and you'll get more intel with an apology," Jacob said.

"So, I should apologize for ditching her?" I asked.

"Don't say it like that, or then she'll know you ditched her." Jacob ran his hands through his hair. "Instead, thank her for dinner and then say that the day finally caught up with you. Leave it at that. Don't lie, but don't offer more than you need to. The day did catch up to you. Hell, none of us would have lasted as long as you did." His green eyes shone with compassion.

"And it didn't help that she questioned Hunter's business

dealings," Reid said. "That would make anybody want to vacate. But she doesn't need to know that, so I'm with Jacob, keep it simple and to the point."

The one person I'd ask for input wasn't on the call. *Hunter*. So, I asked the one guy who had led me on and off the football field.

"Ollie?"

Our former high school and college quarterback's face moved closer to the screen. "Yeah, what's up, buddy?"

"What do you think?"

"I'd be honest. And if that means telling her that she freaked you out asking about your brother, then that's what you tell her," he said. "I don't think Jacob's approach is wrong, I just don't think you're hardwired that way. I'm not. We aren't as good with sharing just the minimum. I think we do better with the straightforward approach."

"Yah, I'd probably forget what I was supposed to say anyway," I said with a laugh. "I've got too many other things to consider, like they're cremating Hunter today." I glanced away and felt my eyes sting.

"Fuck, Hank, that sucks," Jacob said.

I turned toward them and pinched my eyes, but the damage was done. The tears were inevitable. "Yeah." I cleared my throat and lifted my arm to wipe my face against the sleeve of my T-shirt. "It really does."

"Listen, buddy, we can get on a plane right now and be there in a few hours," Ollie said.

I smiled slightly. "Thanks, but this is something I've got to do."

"Just know we're here. Anytime. Any place. Text. Call. E-mail," Ollie said.

"Send one of those owls from Harry Potter," Bryan said, and everyone laughed.

"Thanks, guys," I said. "I'd better go. My parents are waiting for me to drive them to the hospital for the… well, you know what I just said."

No one spoke.

"Whatever you need," Ollie said. "We got your six."

"Thanks."

"Hey, Tank, we love you, buddy," Reid said.

"I love you too, guys." I closed my computer and the familiar ache returned. It was an ache I couldn't imagine would ever go away. Carmen said it took time. I only hoped she was right.

CHAPTER SEVENTEEN

"Georgina, I need your help."

She swiveled in her chair; catlike green eyes lined in heavy black eyeliner looked at me. Rose blush highlighted the apples of her cheeks and complemented her auburn hair. She was lighter skinned than me, with men practically making reservations to take her out, but we grew up together, sharing the same playpen, going to the same Catholic school, and eventually learning to drive together. I knew what most people didn't. Georgie preferred women.

"What's up, *chica*?"

No one was in the IT room, which was housed in the basement; still I glanced in either direction.

"I need to run a virus scan."

"Ohh-kay."

I hesitated, then reached into my pants pocket and handed her the thumb drive.

"My, my, my. What do we have here?" She turned the black device over in her slender fingers like a magician rolling a coin across her knuckles. She popped the cap and held the silver USB interface toward the light. "A MUM stick." Her green eyes flashed in my direction. "What are you doing with this?"

"What's a MUM stick, and how do you know it's a MUM stick?"

Her red acrylic nail pointed to a miniscule marking on the interface. MUM was stamped beside 64 GB.

"What does MUM stand for?"

"Mosby's Unbreakable Memory stick. It can't be hacked or cracked. If you want your data stored safely and securely, MUM's the word."

"Huh. Who's Mosby?"

"The inventor, Stephen Thaddeus, named it after Ted Mosby from *How I Met Your Mother*."

"And it's unbreakable?" I exhaled. "Of course it is. Fantastic."

Georgina continued to stare at the MUM stick. "Nothing's unbreakable. Hell, nothing in the IT world is ever safe. You have Professor Fagan, don't you?"

"I *had* his class. *Chica*, I'm a senior. I'm working on my final capstone project."

"That's right." She turned her attention toward me. "Okay, but do you remember that case study about some of the first encryption algorithms made in 1993 that were all the rave?"

I nodded, mentally recalling the case we studied in class. Professor Fagan was all about using past examples to explain current code.

"So, then you remember how these *ah-mazing* algorithms that seemed like the newest, greatest thing in cyber security, became easily hackable by 1998?"

"I remember that," I said.

"Then you know the way security works. Programmers and coders come up with a technique to safeguard files and systems, but as performance improves it becomes antiquated," she said.

"So, is that what you're saying will happen to the MUM stick? That it'll be hackable? *Or* has someone already figured it out?"

Her head swayed back and forth. "No one's hacked it yet, that I'm aware of, but I'm not convinced it's not possible. The computers in the future will decimate the security protocols we have now."

"Can you hack it?"

She grimaced. "Nothing's impossible, but on an eight-hour shift using a work computer that's constantly monitored, the chances of me hacking it are pretty slim." Georgina capped the thumb drive. "You still haven't told me what you're doing with a MUM stick."

"It's a long story."

She leaned back in her black ergonomic chair and crossed her long legs. "I'm not going anywhere." She glanced at the wall of clocks, in varying time zones, hung above the door. "At least not for another eight hours. Then I have a date with a gal named Trixie."

I couldn't help but smile. "Trixie?"

She shrugged. "If she's as cute as her profile pic, then

I'm aiming to have some fun tonight."

"Be safe."

"Always." She kicked the heel of the mandatory rubber-soled shoe, which she somehow made look fashionable. "Now that we're all caught up, mind telling me what you're doing with this little beauty?"

"I'm sure you heard about that guy that I tried to...." I still wasn't able to discuss Hunter without a knot forming in my throat.

"*Si*. Is this his?"

I nodded.

"And you want to find out what?"

"First, I want to make sure it doesn't contain a virus, then I'm hoping to find out what's on it."

"You're working on your final senior project, right?"

"*Si*."

"So, you've had *some* exposure to decrypting files?" she asked.

"Yeah, not much. But I've done a lot of reading on it."

She slowly shook her head. "Carmen, reading the latest article in *PC World* will not make you an expert. And before you tell me you saw *War Games* or *Snowden*, this isn't some Hollywood movie that makes stealing a thumb drive seem easy and cracking the code easier." She wagged the device at me. "This is the latest in encryption. The only thing you and this stick have in common with what you've read or watched at the movies is that the specialized computer geek you so smartly sought is housed in the basement. They always put us nerds in the basement."

"So, you'll help?"

She pursed her ruby-stained lips together. "I'll try. That's the best I can do."

"Can I watch? My shift doesn't start for another thirty minutes."

"When did you get here?"

"About two hours ago."

"Why would anyone get to the hotel so early?"

I shrugged. "I've been off for a few days. I guess…."

"Entiendo."

"I knew you'd understand. Work may be work, but getting back to some sort of routine helps."

"Pull up a chair. Sid isn't scheduled until my lunch break, so he won't be here for a while."

I wheeled the other ergonomic chair beside her. Georgina was the closest thing I had to a sister. Our families were tight, and our mamás had been even tighter. Georgie was hit hard when Mamá died. She came out to my mamá before coming out to her own.

Georgina held the stick toward the side of the hotel computer. "Portable storage for the paranoid," she mumbled.

"Either that, or he was protecting something or someone," I said.

Her penciled eyebrows rose. "Possibly, but Carmen, someone only uses a MUM stick to store sensitive information or top-secret data. Unlocking it is like Pandora's Box. Once it's open, the secrets are out. Are you sure you want to know what's on here?"

"I do." Maybe Pablo was the paranoid one, or maybe he

was right and whatever was on this flash drive was enough to draw Mr. Harpington out of his deluxe corner office. Either way, I wanted to know.

Georgina plugged the device into the computer. A stream of files popped up and then vanished. "Interesting," she said.

"What happened?"

"It's designed to automatically run a software check by tricking the operating system into thinking I just inserted a CD and not a secure flash drive."

"And it does that to hide the data it contains until it knows the site is secure." I spoke more to myself, but Georgina confirmed my working knowledge of the MUM stick's design.

"Exactly."

"After the MUM stick knows it's in a secure device, it'll run on the control panel once a password is entered."

"Maybe you are learning something at school."

I shook my head. "You're just jealous because soon I'll be sitting down here with you."

She looked at me. "Carmen, I hope you do better than working IT at the hotel. You're a natural with computers. It'd be a shame to waste your talent in the basement."

"But I like cold, dark places."

"Sure, about as much as I like men."

I laughed so hard I snorted, which made Georgina giggle.

"Actually," I said, coming up for air, "thanks to you, I am becoming more fluent in geek-speak, and the numbers and coding down here aren't rude or as demanding as the people upstairs. I got to admit, there's a lot to be said about being kept underground, just as long as it's not a coffin."

She threw her head back and laughed. Her curly reddish hair bounced on her shoulders.

"How come you were blessed with curls and I got stuck with straight hair?"

"If there's one thing I've learned, it's that you've just got to accept yourself as you are, even if a lot of other people refuse to. There's no shame and no one to blame. We're all born the way we are, just like neither my hair, nor me, is straight."

The computer interrupted us to spit code as it checked the hotel's operating system.

"Well, the good news is that MUM stick is designed to install and run off a USB drive, which leaves no footprint on someone's PC. So, we don't have to worry about anyone knowing we accessed it, if we're able to access the files."

"That's brilliant," I said, and leaned toward her. "We think Mr. Harpington is interested in whatever is on here."

"Who's 'we?'" Her fingers danced across the keyboard.

"Pablo from Housekeeping. He's the one who found it in my uniform pocket." Talking to Georgina about Hunter was easier because she knew my heart. She knew what ate at me and kept me up at night. Not being able to do more for Hunter consumed my every thought. If I could present this drive to Hank and save him the time of decrypting it, then hopefully I'd be giving back something of value to him. "When I performed CPR, it was on Hunter's chest. On a lanyard."

Georgina stopped typing. "That's no shit. Hard-core

nerd types will wear a flash drive around their neck when they want to secure something. And if it's dangerous, he would want to keep it on his person."

"You're not making me feel any better about this," I said.

Her face didn't change. "Just forewarning you."

Another string of code surfaced on the computer screen. "Fuck."

"What?" I tried to follow the line of code, but I wasn't sure I understood it correctly.

"Well, not only did he use a MUM stick, but it looks like he added a polymorphic encryption to it."

"Uh…." I mentally cataloged my course work. "That's what? An algorithm that changes with each device the flash drive is plugged into?"

"Exactly. He *really* didn't want anyone to access his files. However, there's an upside." Her red nail pointed to a keyboard that materialized on the screen. "The encryption provides a virtual keyboard to prevent key-logging programs from stealing the password when and if we're able to break it."

"But it looks like the hotel's software is interacting with the drive?"

"It is, and so far no virus has been detected, on either side—his MUM stick or our system. Not that I expected there to be one. He went to a lot of trouble to secure whatever's on here. He wouldn't have risked a virus."

"Damn. Is there *any* downside to a MUM stick?"

"The cost." She nodded toward the computer and the black stick protruding from the side. "That little sleek stick costs in the neighborhood of four to five hundred."

"Nun-uh."

"Uh-huh."

"Wow."

"It does have sixty-four gigabytes, so it can hold a shit ton of extremely secure info, but it ain't cheap," Georgina said.

"You're not kidding me. Who knew the thumb drive I stuffed in my pocket was that pricey."

"And fast. For a portable encrypted drive, it's far faster with large files than you'd think. And whatever he put on here was undoubtedly a big file. The MUM stick, though, is a real time saver, which is most likely why he used it. It would have allowed him to work directly off the drive without ever having his confidential data reside in another location. Unless he moved a copy to a secure online backup service, which he probably did. But trying to find that would be like trying to find a yellow brick in Kansas."

"Yeah, I'm not thinking that's going to happen."

"We need to write our own polymorphic self-decryption code to crack this," Georgina said.

"Or...."

She glanced at me. "What?"

"I remember one of my professors said something about how security lies in the knowledge of the key, not the algorithm. If we could reconstruct the changing key he's figured into his algorithm...."

"Then we'd be able to eliminate the key and decrypt the code."

"Exactly," I said.

"Damn, *chica*, you do know your shit."

"It's one thing to know it, but an entirely different thing to implement it."

"Well, let's start simply and see where we get." She typed a polymorphic self-decryption code. The computer instantly responded.

decryption key; 4 bytes decrypted?

"Four? We have sixty more bytes to decrypt?" I glanced at the clock in Pacific time. "Shit. I've got to get to my shift."

"Listen, I'll work on this until Sid relieves me." She flipped her wrist and checked her watch. Georgina started her college career in nursing and hadn't broken the habit of wearing her watch upside down to time a pulse. "I'll set an alarm and shut down before he arrives. I'll bring you what I have. But you'll probably have to do the rest on your own, unless I get really lucky."

I wrapped my arm around her and squeezed. "Gracias. Now to go train the owner's nephew."

"I'd rather sit in the dark, decrypting code." She laughed. "Me too."

CHAPTER **EIGHTEEN**

One car was ahead of mine. A father, mother, and a carful of towheaded children bounded from the maroon minivan that showed its miles. Dried mud and dust covered the tailgate. "Wash Me" was written in the layer of grime that coated the rear window. The out-of-state license plates made me smile. *Family vacation.*

With my window rolled down, the breeze off the Pacific cooled the bundle of nerves tightening my gut. *Apologize. It's that simple.* Yet my stomach jumped when Carmen came into view.

The mother and older children headed toward the hotel, while the father and youngest child, a little girl, remained with the car.

"We're going to Disneyland!" Her pigtails were tied with pink ribbons, and a stuffed white bunny was tucked beneath her arm.

Carmen knelt before the little girl.

"Disneyland! Ay Dios mio!"

"What does that mean?"

"It means she's the help." The lanky, middle-aged man with thinning blond hair hurried his daughter away from Carmen as if she had a disease. The bunny lay in the wake of his outburst.

"What was she speaking, Daddy?"

His response was spoken loudly and curtly. "Mexican."

Anyone in the carport heard.

I grabbed the handle and pushed a bit too hard against the car door, but it had the desired effect. When I stepped out of the rental, the man and little girl turned in my direction. I walked toward them and reached for the bunny.

When I rose, I studied the man and looked down at the six-foot nothing. "Her name's Carmen, and she speaks Spanish, *not Mexican*, quite beautifully." I handed the bunny to his daughter while keeping him locked in my sights. "She's not the help, she's a college student, valet, and most recently a hero."

"Hero?" The disdain was palpable.

"She came to my brother's rescue when he was choking."

The man tried to dismiss me, but I blocked his exit.

"And you owe her an apology."

He gave me his best version of a badass stare, so I took a step toward him and my chest consumed what little space there was between us. "It's actually pretty simple. In fact, I'll help you. All you have to say is, 'I'm sorry for being an insensitive prick.'"

"Daddy, why is your hand sweaty?"

I grinned and raised my eyebrow. "That's what I thought."

I cocked my head toward Carmen, whose mouth was agape, her blue eyes as wide as quarters. "Let's hear it."

The man's jaw tightened, and my fists clenched. I leaned toward him and lowered my voice to barely a whisper. "Whatever you're thinking, not a good idea."

He glared, then dragged his daughter by the wrist toward Carmen. "I'd like to…."

I took a step toward him.

"Apologize," he said.

Carmen looked from him to me. I arched an eyebrow, as if to ask if his apology met with her approval. Carmen nodded in return.

"Sir, will you be checking any bags this afternoon?" she said.

It was the first time the man showed any embarrassment. His face flushed and he fumbled with his words. "Uh, yeah, they're in the—"

"Car! Daddy put all the luggage in the back seat." The girl pulled away from her father and wrapped her arms around Carmen's legs. "Thank you! We're going to Disneyland!"

Her father turned from Carmen, and I stood my ground behind him. "Aren't you forgetting something?"

His dark eyes searched my face for an answer. "I apologized."

"She's getting your bags." I glanced at the rear of his minivan. "And from the looks of it, she's got quite a lot to unload."

"Yeah, so?"

The man was either stupid or cheap, and I knew how to

correct the latter. I raised two fingers and slowly rubbed my thumb back and forth across them in the universal gesture for money, and nodded toward Carmen.

I planted my hands on my hips, turned my head to loudly crack my neck, and gave him a hard stare with cold eyes. I uttered not a single word, but my body language spoke volumes. When I left this morning in my extra, extra, extra large University of Oregon jersey, I may have looked like the Jolly Green Giant, but now with my expression, I probably more resembled the Incredible Hulk. He was either going to give her a healthy tip or, as Charles Darwin would theorize, he was just too dumb to survive.

He pulled his wallet from his khaki slacks and handed Carmen two twenties.

"Enjoy Disneyland," I said, and heartily patted him on his back.

###

Ohhhhhhh. Damn.

Bryce ran and grabbed the suitcase I'd dropped. "I'll take care of the bags."

I barely nodded.

Hank stepped toward me. "I was hoping to run into you today."

I stared into the greenish-brown eyes that swirled together like his brother's, but instead of spinning me for a loop, they bored into my heart. Hard.

"Carmen?"

I heard Hank, but I couldn't respond. *I'm falling for a giant.*

He gently touched my shoulder with a massive hand. "You okay?"

"No one's ever done that." Suddenly I felt like a young girl. I wrapped my arms around him—or what I could of his waist. "You're my hero."

He tipped my chin toward him, looked longingly into my eyes, lowered his head, and softly kissed me. His lips melded into mine, his heart beat against me, and my body responded, pressing into him with a mixture of tenderness and desire that had no beginning and no end.

"Gonzalez!"

Nothing like hearing my surname bellowed across the front drive to completely kill a romantic moment. Time of death, 12:35 p.m.

I pulled away from Hank, but not before staring into his eyes. "I don't want you to vanish again." I finally let my heart and not my head speak. "I don't want you to leave."

A devil-may-care grin crossed his face. "Now, who said *anything* about goodbye?"

CHAPTER NINETEEN

"Okay, shit just got serious." Georgina discreetly tucked the MUM stick into my pants pocket. "If this Hunter guy was as concerned about his security as I think he was, my guess is he had another backup."

"Why? What happened?" I kept my focus on Bryce, who met a guest in front of his red BMW. The personalized plates on the Beemer read "TBone."

"Does that say…?" Georgina followed my gaze.

I laughed. "Apparently, Bryce will be checking TBone and his car."

"Who does that?"

"*Chica*, you'd be surprised. People's cars are akin to their alter egos. If we can't be what we want or imagine ourselves as, then we may as well drive the image of the person we truly wish to project."

"What did this guy drive?" She lightly tugged on the side seam of my pocket.

"A Mercedes. It was an older model with a stick shift,

which I think is sexy as hell. Yeah." I nodded, remembering Hunter's car. "It was a sleek, silver, smooth Mercedes—just like his personality."

"Is his car still here?"

I turned toward her. "Yeah… it is."

Her ruby lips curved into a smile. "*Bueno.* If Hunter had a backup it'd either be in his car or he may have left something in his car that would lead us to it."

"What makes you so convinced Hunter had a backup, and if he did that it'd be in his car?" I asked.

"You said Hunter had the MUM stick on a lanyard around his neck, right?"

I nodded.

"So, he kept the MUM stick on his person, but most computer nerds have a backup system in the event they lose their MUM stick. I can tell from trying to decrypt the MUM stick that Hunter was working overtime to protect his shit, which is why I don't doubt he had something else as a backup. A fail-safe. The key is to get inside his car and take a look," Georgina said. "Hunter was way too smart to leave it at the Waterfront Point. My guess is his car."

"But Hank's here."

"That's his brother, right?"

I nodded. "He showed up about an hour ago in a powerfully tough, untamed, metallic blue, sporty Mustang that had a throttle like you wouldn't believe." My body revved and I felt my face light into a smile.

"Are we still talking about his car?"

"Anyway." I exhaled, and on the inhale the salty air

filled my lungs. "So, when Hank arrived, this guest was being rude—" I rolled my eyes. "—like *that* never happens. But he totally got in the guy's face."

"What'd the guy do?"

I tilted my head. "Hank?'

"No, the rude guy."

I pointed to the double-wide glass doors that the bellman opened for Hank.

"That's him," I said, still dumbstruck that the tall, rugged man had kissed me.

"Seriously? The guy in the jersey?" Her tone was as surprised as the expression on her face.

"Oh yeah. That's Hank. Hank the Tank."

"Indeed."

Hank walked toward us, wearing faded blue jeans, his University of Oregon jersey, and a grin that made my stomach somersault.

"Hello again," he said, as if Georgina weren't even there. It was a first for both of us. Everyone noticed Georgie.

"Hola."

"Hey," Georgina addressed him curtly.

"Hey." Hank softened the edge.

"My *chica* here told me about the rude guy." Georgina crossed her arms over her chest. We didn't share any blood, but damn if we weren't connected.

Hank slowly nodded.

"What'd this guy do?" she asked.

"Georgie, it was nothing I'm not used to. He made a comment to his daughter that I was the help and spoke

'Mexican.' You know, typical small-minded bigotry that, unfortunately, is inflicted on others by insensitive people of all races, religions, and genders."

Georgina glanced toward Hank. "Thanks for being there for Carm." She pivoted back to me. "I get that you've conditioned yourself to shrug off insults, but this guy sounds like a douche."

"He was." Hank placed his hands on his hips, and unlike when Bogart did it, Hank's mannerism had impact. The man was a sexy beast, and I couldn't take my eyes off him.

"And no one, least of all Carmen, should be subjected to him. To me, there's nothing typical about it. I still don't get used to being called 'big and dumb,' so you must be a far better person to forgive those who call you something far worse."

"Thanks, Hank," I said, "but it's not that I'm a better person. I still get offended and imagine hiding a bag of compost in his trunk. But there's no win. If I even *hint* at being singled out because I'm Latina, the issue suddenly becomes 'rational racism.' A guy like the one you saw today would be the first to remind me that *if* there was any racism," my forefinger spliced the air like a wand, "it's equally balanced between *all* the minorities. I wasn't being singled out because racism doesn't discriminate. With that logic, I'm just supposed to accept whatever ill treatment comes my way because it's rational. Which is why it's just easier to ignore assholes and idiots."

"I won't. In fact, that's the biggest load of cowshit I've ever heard. People actually say stuff like that and think it makes things better?"

"Rational racism—it's a thing. A way to make other people feel better about their poor choices," I said.

"I'm not denying it's real, but if it happens again, I'm going to say something. It's not right," Hank said.

Georgina wasn't a fan of any man that showed interest in me, but Hank wasn't any man. She studied him and then smiled. "You're okay, Hank."

Yes, he is. I smiled in his direction. "So," I said, and then didn't know how to finish. *So, are you staying in California? So... what happens now? So... how far is Oregon from California anyway?*

"So," he said, grinning.

Georgina stood to the side of our attraction that brimmed with energy, heat, uncertainty, and a whole lot of curiosity.

"Hey, Hank?" Georgina said.

It was the only time he broke eye contact with me. "Yah. It's Georgie, right?"

She nodded. "Or Georgina. But either works. I was wondering if you'd be okay if we checked out your brother's car?"

"His car?" He looked from Georgina to me. "His car is in Oregon."

"Maybe it was a rental?" I said.

"Of course. I didn't even think about a car. Yeah, is it still here?" he asked.

"It is. I hadn't thought about it until Georgie asked." I tilted my head toward her. "She thinks maybe your brother left a second backup in his car or evidence of a backup? You know, for security reasons."

Hank was about to respond when Bryce walked into our semicircle and aimed his attention directly at Georgina. "Hi. I'm Bryce. And you are?"

"Not interested."

I burst out laughing and covered my mouth with my hand. "Georgie!"

"Sorry, kid, but stick with checking out cars. I think you'll have better luck," she said. "Besides, it's time for Carmen's break, and my *chica* has something for me in her car." She glanced at me and her voice shifted to playful and light. "Carmen, did you hang your car keys in the valet box again?"

I was about to shake my head when it registered. "Right." I slapped my forehead for good measure. "I know we're not supposed to leave our personal keys in the box," I directed to Bryce, "but with these pants there's no room for anything more than a tissue." *And a MUM stick.*

"Yeah, who came up with these uniforms anyway? We look like we're at a *really* bad wedding where everyone's a groomsman, including the women."

Richard walked into the conversation, and Hank subtly walked away.

"Now, Bryce, you don't look anything like a groomsman. The uniforms present a well-groomed man, and woman, here to help usher in our guests."

"Still, sounds like the wedding from hell, but at least we don't have to buy a gift," Bryce said to a shocked Richard. No one ever countered Dick.

"It's Carmen's meal break, so does that mean it's mine too?" Bryce said.

I smiled. *Ah, he remembered to use Richard speak and call it a meal, not lunch or dinner.*

Richard reached into his navy jacket pocket and withdrew a schedule that he unfolded. While he reviewed it, I looked for Hank. For a big guy, he could quickly disappear like Houdini in his prime. He stood across from the hotel on a side street. He was in a perfect position for me to pick him up in his brother's rental. *Maybe there's a Prince concert we could sneak off to?* I smiled.

"Well, I suppose I could cover the drive. You have an hour, no more, no less."

"Actually, my uncle wanted to take me to a long lunch with the General Manger," Bryce said and Richard frowned.

"All right two hours, but this is highly unusual." Richard turned to me. "Will this conflict with your training schedule?" he asked.

I shook my head. "Not at all."

"Very well then," Richard said. "You can both take a two-hour meal break, but just so you know," he wagged his finger at Bryce, "you won't get paid for the extra meal hour."

"Got it, thanks! I'll let my uncle know. I'm sure he'll appreciate your flexibility," Bryce said, and darted toward the hotel.

The boy is good, I'll give him that. I glanced at Georgina and then toward the key box. She positioned herself in front of Richard. "Hey, Richard! How the heck are you? Have you been working out?" She touched his forearm. "Oh, you have, haven't you?"

She really knew how to charm a man, which was such a waste of talent. I couldn't charm a man even if I were covered in pizza slices and wore nothing but a widescreen TV that played nothing but all sports all the time.

I slipped out of the circle and grabbed the keys hung on the bottom hook. When I didn't know Hunter's last name, I'd placed them on the hook that wasn't designated to a room. If anyone searched for keys to Hunter's car by his room number, they'd come up empty. And if they looked for his silver Mercedes, they'd also get nowhere. I'd parked his car in the one place no one would look—in plain sight. It was one of the showcase cars we parked to the side of the front drive. I held the keys in Georgina's line of vision and cocked my head toward the Mercedes.

"Richard, do you have your workout routine on your computer?" She looped her arm through his and directed them toward the hotel. "I know you're supposed to cover the front, but my break *just* finished," she said loud enough for me to hear. "But I can't leave without knowing your fitness secret. Would you mind *file sharing* it with me? Then we could *tail* each other's progress."

Richard's cheeks glowed like Rudolph's nose. "Oh, it's really nothing."

Georgina swatted his arm. "Now, now, the proof's in the pudding. Just think, we can *merge our files and tail the outcome.* Doesn't that sound fun?" She quickly glanced in my direction.

File sharing. Tail filing? What the hell? Whatever was on the MUM stick had to do with file sharing, tail filing, or maybe Georgie wanted to get some tail. I had no clue, but I knew where I could find the answer. While Georgina and Richard disappeared into the hotel, I slipped inside the Mercedes.

CHAPTER **TWENTY**

"So, when your brother…." I again found myself starting a thought I wasn't prepared to complete. "Uh…."

"Died. Hunter died. It's okay to say it aloud."

For a moment, I glanced away from the traffic on Pacific Coast Highway and toward Hank, who barely fit in the passenger seat.

"Right. When he died, or actually before that, when I performed CPR, there was something on a lanyard around his neck."

"His MUM stick."

"Yeah. I totally forgot about it because I put it in my pants pocket and went back trying to…."

"Save his life."

When I exhaled, the hollow, empty feeling from losing Hunter settled in the pit of my stomach. I knew Hank's pain was deeper and cut wider than anything I felt. When Mamá died, Georgina was sad, but she still had her mamá. Her loss wasn't even close or comparable to mine. How could it be? I lost my mamá, just like Hank lost his brother. There were some losses that no one felt as deeply as you. I gently placed my hand on his, and he interlocked our fingers. I didn't know how we fit, only that we did.

"I have his MUM stick. The laundry department gave it back to me versus giving it to Mr. Harpington, who apparently seemed *really* interested in it or anything computer related to your brother."

"I bet." Hank gently released my hand and rolled his shoulders into the leather seat. "The guy's a major puke. I went to get Hunter's belongings and he wasn't there, so his secretary wouldn't release them to me. Can you believe that?"

"Actually, I can."

"His secretary asked if I'd come back later because they have paperwork for my parents to sign to hold the hotel harmless in his death. Piece of shit."

"Pinche cabrón." I gripped the steering wheel and dug my ocean-inspired navy-painted nails into the padded leather. I wanted to tap my fingertips together three times while saying "There's no place like the beach" and hope the car suddenly brought us there, but I had to get Hank and the MUM stick to campus before my two-hour lunch went beyond its allotted time and turned into unemployment.

"I know we don't have a lot of time before you have to get back on your shift," he said. "But do you think we could get my brother's MUM stick?"

"Actually, I lucked out and got an extra hour on my lunch. And…." I leaned against my seat, but I couldn't raise myself high enough to get into my pants pocket. Besides, it'd probably take two hands—one to hold the waistband to make the pocket stretch, and the other to reach into it. The pants had absolutely no pocket depth, so items got stuck in the corner of the seam.

"Whoever made these pants must have thought shallow pockets was the best way to keep employees' hands out of their pockets. As if we had nothing but time on our hands and nothing better to do than keep them in our pockets," I said.

Confusion settled on Hank's face.

"Oh, yeah. I probably should have led with the fact that I have the MUM stick." I scrunched my face. "But it's in my pants pocket. Can you get it?"

"Uh… sure." Hank dipped his forefinger into the corner of my pants, feeling his way toward the MUM stick. His eyes searched my face, and if I hadn't been driving, I would have answered his question. *Yes. Yes, I want you. Yes, I know it makes no sense. Yes, my pants are really tight.*

The heat and energy that soared from his finger made me lose concentration. I shook my head and focused on the stretch of highway that could take us all the way to Mexico if we wanted to escape. The warmth of his finger caused my hip to instinctively rise toward his touch. I'd love to think it was to help him retrieve his brother's memory stick, but it wasn't that altruistic. I wanted Hank's finger all over me. Hell, I wanted his hands to rip apart my tuxedo shirt, pull off my slacks, and ravage me. His hands were massive; I could only imagine other body parts. Muy caliente.

He cleared his throat. "Wow, this pocket, these pants… huh.…"

"Uh-huh."

Neither of us were capable of more than a mutter. His finger was so thick it felt like an entire hand. My heart raced, my cheeks flushed, and the temperature in the car spiked.

"Is… uh, is it hot in here?" he asked.

I focused on his eyes, and then moved down to his lips then back to his eyes. "Little bit."

"You smell like the beach," he said.

I nodded and tried to stay in my lane, but I kept veering toward the rumble strips on the shoulder of the road. Each time the car bumped across them, it reminded me I was entering a part of the terrain I hadn't intended.

"I mean you smell *amazing*."

The car's vibration caused me to readjust and stay on course. "It's coconut lotion. Keeps my skin smooth, not ashy," I said, as matter-of-factly as I could muster with his finger in my pocket.

His other hand swept a stray hair from my face and tucked it behind my ear. "Your skin is as exotic as your eyes."

A sudden honk snapped me forward to our surroundings. I quickly veered back to my lane. *Dear God, I'm going to kill us.* Thankfully the upcoming light from Pacific Coast Highway onto Newport Boulevard turned red. I fell in line behind a row of cars.

Nervous laughter filled the space between us. "Sorry about that," Hank said. "I'm just having a really hard time getting into your pants." His cheeks flushed red and his clarification only made it worse. "I mean, I'm just so big and it's a *really* tight squeeze."

Yeah, it is. I didn't know if the light had changed because I couldn't take my eyes off Hank. His face went from a slight blush to lobster red.

"No, I mean… you know, that's what I meant, I was just…." But before he could finish his babbling, and his train of thought, the light turned green, but the car completely stopped.

Shit. "I stalled the car." My brain went to mush at the exact moment his did. Sweaty hands made it difficult to turn the key in the ignition. Hank steadied my hand with his, and together we started the car.

"If I take my eyes off the road one more time, we'll be in bed a lot sooner than expected, but it'll be either in the emergency room or the morgue."

He grinned. "So maybe I shouldn't try to get in your fancy pants?"

"Is it bad that I don't want you to stop?" I put the Mercedes in first and joined the train of cars headed up the hill that led to campus. The road curved, and his finger gripped my hip bone like a pair of lobster claws, which was the shade his entire face became. My flirting knew no end because my attraction to him was just beginning.

When the road smoothed, along with my driving, Hank fingered his way through my pocket. "Got it." He held up the sleek memory stick, and I think we were both disappointed his game of seek and find had ended. "Yup, this is Hunter's."

"Ohh-kay, I know it's Hunter's, but how do you?"

Hank pulled the protective cap off the stick and glanced at it. "Yup, it's his. Hunter always engraved an *O* on the silver USB interface."

"An *O*, as in the letter in the alphabet?"

"As in Oregon, the University of Oregon, and as Hunter would say, 'O, you best leave my shit alone.'" Hank chuckled with the memory.

"I didn't see that. I brought it to Georgina, who works in IT, to see if we could find out what was on it." I realized that probably came out wrong so I quickly waved my hand. "I swear I wasn't snooping. I was curious after Pablo in housekeeping told me Mr. Harpington asked about a thumb drive or hard drive in your brother's hotel room. But my intention wasn't to snoop or invade your brother's privacy. I wanted to print or download whatever Hunter last worked on so you'd have it. I thought it might be helpful."

"I already know what's on the MUM stick."

"Oh." My foot stepped off the gas pedal and the car began to lose speed. "Then we don't need to go to the college." I looked for a section of road to turn around. "That's where I was taking us, because it's encrypted with an algorithm that changes every time the stick is plugged into a new device. But if you know what's on it, then there's no need to decrypt it." I flipped on my signal light.

"Actually, there is." Hank wagged the MUM stick. "I have a vague idea of what's on this. But if Mr. Harpington wants my folks to sign off on a hold harmless agreement, then I want to make sure there's nothing to hold the hotel and Mr. Harpington harmful for."

I pressed on the gas and switched off my turn signal. "We can try to find out what's on here. Georgina worked on it byte by byte to eliminate the key and decrypt the code."

I switched lanes and glanced at Hank.

"I'm confusing you," I said.

"Kind of."

"Okay, so Hunter not only used a MUM stick, but he also added a polymorphic algorithm that makes it nearly impossible to open the files he stored on the stick, because the code constantly mutates."

"Ohh-kay."

"Basically, the code changes each time the stick runs, but the function of the code doesn't change." I rapped my fingers against the steering wheel, thinking of a way to explain something that made perfect sense to me. But computer speak was my third language. "Okay, so we know that one plus three, and six minus two, both have the same result or the same variable, right?"

"Sure, they both equal four."

"Right. So that's what your brother did with the MUM stick when he wrote the algorithm. He encrypted his file or files with random encryption commands that generate or mutate code each time the device is plugged in. However, by breaking the program language byte by byte, we'll be able to reconstruct the variable or key he figured into his algorithm."

"Like the number four."

"Exactly."

"Wouldn't you just need to break one byte to find the variable, because won't all the variables be the same for the rest of the bytes?"

"That's a great question." I meant it. Hank was no dummy. "But there's also something called shell codes that hide their presence and make it appear to be the code we're looking for, but it's really more like a shell game. Where is the code? Is it under this shell in byte five, or beneath this shell in byte six?"

"Which is why you have to break each byte to find the pattern?"

"Exactly. Your brother used a key, but the key is in code. So, different versions of the same code are imbedded on the disk. Like different ways to arrive at the number four. There's two plus two, three plus one, six minus two, four times one, and you get the idea. They all equal four, so each version of the code allows the stick to function the same, but it's discovering the main body of the code, or payload, that will decrypt the stick and allow it to function."

Hank held the silver USB interface toward the windshield. "Sixty-four bytes?"

I cringed. "Yeah, that's what I thought too." Then I chuckled. "It seems like a Hughes trait—you guys don't do anything small."

He laughed. "Or in moderation. We don't know how to quit."

Hell yeah. I hope he doesn't know how to quit, because I could lose a few hours just undressing him. I cleared my throat and tried to swallow the naughty thoughts that raced through my mind.

"So, I'm not sure how many bytes Georgina broke. But before I left she mentioned file sharing or tail filing? She completely lost me. I know she was trying to get a message to me. I'll text her when we get on campus."

"No need to text. It's called tailing the file." Hank hit the dashboard with his palm. "Hunter and I talked about it while he was eating dinner."

"Tailing the file? Wait." I rubbed my forehead and wished I could close my eyes to concentrate on a lecture I'd attended on program files.

"I think it's also called something like tail…." Hank's hand opened like he was trying to catch the memory of his last conversation with his brother. "Tail…."

"Tail… minus f!" I whacked the steering wheel. "F is the command line. The f stands for follow, because the program updates files in real time."

"That's it."

The red-and-white entrance sign to the college came into view. "Did your brother want to tail some file?"

"Oh, yah."

"Really? Why? Who was he tailing?"

Hank didn't miss a beat. "Mr. Harpington."

"What?" I wanted to pull over, but I knew we had a mission to complete and time was against us. Instead, I fell in line behind a row of cars waiting to turn into the campus lot, and pointed toward a gray brick structure in the distance. "The computer lab is in that building." I turned to Hank. "Why would your brother want to tail Mr. Harpington?

What was he doing?"

"Mr. Harpington asked Hunter to install a program that allowed him to see what information employees accessed online."

"Like our buying habits? He can do that by just checking our browser history."

Hank held the MUM stick. "No, because I thought basically the same thing. But Hunter said that Mr. Harpington wasn't interested in what employees accessed online, he wanted to *know* what people did *online* while they were doing it. Apparently there's a big difference."

"Uh, yeah. With one you're just securing your site so that malware and other viruses aren't accidentally downloaded in a search. But he was basically tailing our files to know in real time what people were doing. In short, he asked your brother to create an online surveillance of the staff without our knowledge or consent. This would have given Mr. Harpington access to personal e-mail accounts, bank statements—anything an employee accessed, Mr. Harpington could too, as it happened. That's creepy as shit."

"I agree, which is why Hunter installed his own program to monitor Mr. Harpington's activity."

"Nice."

"I know." Hank held the MUM stick and turned to me. "And Georgina wanted to know if my brother's car was still here because she thought he left something behind?"

"Yup, like a hard drive? Or maybe another MUM stick?"

Hank glanced over his shoulder. "There's nothing in the back seat."

"We can check the trunk when we get on campus. It's a long shot," I said.

"Not really. Hunter said something about having a security backup offsite, so maybe he was referring to his car."

When the oncoming traffic cleared a path, I pulled into the college parking lot, cut a sharp turn toward the business administration building, and instinctively reached for the glove box, only to realize this wasn't my car. "Damn! I don't have my student parking pass."

Hank's laughter startled me. "I'm not real concerned about a ticket. It's a rental, but if one's left on the windshield, I'll add it to the bill. As long as you don't park in a handicap slot. That's messed up."

"Agreed." I aimed for the back parking where the campus security rarely visited. The farther the walk, the less the motivation.

"But it makes you wonder…." Hank pressed the chrome button on the glove box console and it silently fell open. He lowered his head and thumbed through the contents. "Owner's manual. Rental agreement. Room key."

"Room key?" I cut the engine, and Hank handed me the plastic key fob. "This isn't for our hotel." I gave it back to him.

"Are you sure? It looks like the one I have."

We stared at each other and our faces registered the same shocked look. "Where's your hotel key?" I asked.

Hank unbuckled, reached into his jeans pocket, and withdrew a key card that was an identical match to the one in the glovebox of his brother's rental.

"Oh. My. Hell. You're right, it is a hotel room key, but not to the Waterfront. It's a key to our biggest competitor, the Newport Heights."

"What was my brother doing with a room key to *that* hotel?"

I slowly shook my head. "I don't know. Maybe he uncovered something tailing Mr. Harpington before he died? Could that be possible? Or am I beginning to sound paranoid?"

Hank held the two card keys side by side. "There's nothing paranoid about this. Hunter died sometime before ten, because he called me a few hours after his six o'clock dinner meeting with Mr. Harpington. Only the bastard never fed him, which is why Hunter ordered room service."

"Well, Katie and I wanted to buy time from my shift so we delayed going to Hunter's room till nine-ish. Or nine thirty? We started playing online scrabble." I shook my head. "It was stupid but neither of us wanted to resume our real jobs and that game is crazy addicting. So, Katie phoned Richard, my supervisor, that we were almost through and that's when we headed toward your brother's room. I think we got to his room between nine and nine thirty." This time I closed my eyes and thought back to the night Hunter died. Katie was working late on a project, which was why she was able to help me. Then she staked claim to an hour of my time when Richard wanted me back on my shift, which ended at ten. "That's right." I popped open my eyes. "I had two hours left on my shift. I worked the two to ten. If

Hunter's dinner meeting was at six and we went to his room at nine-ish, that leaves at least two full hours unaccounted for. Would that have been enough time for your brother to make software adjustments for Mr. Harpington and tail his file?"

Hank grinned. "My brother came up with the idea for FrogKiss at an intermission at a Grateful Dead concert. He wrote the program the next day. Yah, he could update software and tail Mr. Harpington with his hands tied behind his back and his eyes closed. My brother was a computer genius."

I softly smiled. "Yeah, he was. But it still begs the question, what was he doing with a room key for Newport Heights?"

Hank put both card keys in his back pocket and reached for the door handle. "I'm not sure. Maybe if we know for sure what's on the MUM stick, we'll have a better idea."

I reached for the car keys in the ignition, and Hank was out before I set the parking brake. For a big guy, he moved quickly.

"If Georgina was talking about the tail minus f program, do you think she got into his files?" He spoke over his shoulder.

I ran to catch up. "Maybe, I'm not sure. Besides Mr. Harpington, did your brother want to tail someone else?"

Hank shrugged. "I'm not sure. No one that he mentioned."

"Really?" It felt like my heart would beat out of my chest for how fast I walked to keep step beside him. "He didn't mention anyone else? The hotel is known for behind-closed-doors board meetings that only benefit the board."

"No, he only mentioned Mr. Harpington."

I wanted to pause and catch my breath, but Hank moved too quickly. I pointed toward the entrance. "The computer lab is downstairs."

He held the door, and as I passed I shot another question his way. "If he wanted to tail Mr. Harpington because he was watching us, maybe in tailing him he found something."

"Possibly."

I swung open the door to the computer lab, and the blinds on the back side rattled against the glass.

"What's with these?" Hank tugged on the vinyl shades.

"It prevents the glare from the hallway lights. They're blackout shades. After an hour of writing code, any light can be too much. The shades filter light and better yet, no one can peer in and watch us like we're in a fishbowl."

"Cool."

The classroom was empty. The wall clock read 1:10 p.m., which was in the middle of most afternoon classes. "We'll probably be alone until we leave to return to the hotel. Or rather, *I* have to get back to the hotel."

"No, you were right." Hank commandeered two gray, padded chairs and placed them before a computer at the back of the room. "It's no longer 'I' or 'me,' it's 'we' and 'us.' Sorry to break it to you, fancy pants, but we're in this together."

CHAPTER **TWENTY-ONE**

"Who knew this little MUM stick was a veritable Swiss Army knife of tools and utilities." Carmen inserted what looked to the naked eye like a typical USB thumb drive into the side of the computer.

"Yeah, MUM sticks are pretty badass," I said. "My brother swore by them."

"I get it. He loaded this stick with all sorts of fly programs. He could safely browse the web, check his e-mail, and from what Georgina texted, he could even edit his photos regardless of what was installed on the PC he was plugged into. Your brother is a genius." No sooner did the words leave her mouth then her eyes widened. "Oh, Hank, I wasn't thinking."

"Carmen, it's okay. What *wasn't* okay was watching my parents sign the paperwork to cremate my brother." My arms extended out in front of me and then quickly swept outward, palms down, like an umpire calling safe in baseball. Although there was nothing safe about knowing my brother would return home to Oregon in an urn. "I *never* want to go through that again." I cut the air with my hands. "Anyway, I had to get out of that hospital, so this is a welcome reprieve. In fact," I glanced at the room full of computers in varying shapes, sizes, and systems, "This is the best place for me to be—in Hunter's element. Shit—" I chuckled. "—this would have been a candy store for him."

"I bet, right?" While she waited for the MUM stick to load, she brushed her hair back with her fingers and twisted it into a rope she tied behind her head.

The computer spit something onto the screen, and her eyes narrowed, reading the code.

"I'm not sure I'll be any help," I said.

"Hopefully I won't need any." She smiled without looking at me. When I first saw Carmen in my brother's hospital room, her profile captivated me. Now I was close enough to touch her delicate features, but I didn't.

"Hey, I wanted to apologize for ditching you on the beach like that," I said, opting for the straightforward, no-bullshit approach.

She stopped typing and turned toward me. A soft smile lit her face. "So, you *did* ditch me."

I rolled my shoulders like I was preparing for a hit in football. "Yeah, it wasn't the right move, but I freaked out when questions about Hunter's business and what he was doing at the hotel surfaced."

She leaned against her chair. "I'd want to ditch me too. I hadn't even considered all my questions and how that must have made you feel. No wonder you left."

She wore little makeup, but there was no need. Her caramel-colored skin and blue eyes were a startling contrast I couldn't stop noticing. I'd seen many beautiful women on the beach outside my hotel room. *Hell, the Beach Boys weren't lying about California girls.* But unlike the blonde, golden, leggy goddesses that seemed to multiply along the shore, Carmen's beauty was breathtaking, in that she literally took my breath away.

"Eh, it is what it is. You were curious. That makes sense. But that doesn't erase how I handled it, and for that I am sorry," I said.

Her stare flickered down to my crotch and then to my face with a grin. "Wow. Most men can't utter those three little words without fear of their dick falling off."

I laughed. "And what three words would those be?"

She leaned toward me, and her blue eyes flashed against her dark features. "I. Am. Sorry."

"Well, *I. Am. Sorry.*" I jokingly cupped my cock. "And it's still here."

Her neck turned crimson. "Good to know," she said, and the dimples that appeared every time she smiled brought me to my knees. Her eyes always twinkled before she laughed, and I knew from the sparkle in her eyes that giggling was about to ensue. "Ha! Good to know." She elbowed me, chuckling. "Another three-word winner."

"Wanna get naked?"

She shrieked and covered her mouth with her hand. "Hank!" Her accent came out with certain words, and the way she said my name made it sound like hunk, which was fine by me. "Naked?" She couldn't stop giggling and fanning herself. "Ay Dios mio!"

"Chill. I'm just playing with another three-word sentiment."

Her silky black hair fell from its knot, swaying, and shone like wet paint. She turned her attention to the computer. "If I don't get busy, we're going to have to return tonight."

"A night alone in a computer lab. That's my go-to Friday night date." I moved toward her. "And more time with you. Oh, the many three-worded things I'd like to do. How 'bout you?"

She kept her focus on the computer, but her dimples answered for her.

"Well, my offer stands. If we don't have time to hack his MUM stick, I seriously wouldn't mind coming back with you."

Her blue-painted index finger and thumb nails shot toward me like a gun. "What did you just say?"

I shook my head. "Uh, that we could come back tonight?"

"No, before that you said something about hacking." Her beautiful, slender hands barely touched the keys when she typed. Everything about Carmen was a light touch. Her blue eyes brightened. "We've been trying to decrypt the MUM stick when maybe, possibly, we could just hack it?" Carmen didn't sound convinced.

"Can you do that?" I studied the computer but the code on the screen was Greek to me. "And *how* would you do that?"

"Well, Georgina said 'nothing's unbreakable,' which got

me thinking about this case study we learned in one of my IT classes. Professor Fagan always said, 'The weakest link point will be human.'"

"What does that mean?" I asked.

"It means that in respect to computer security, a human created the MUM stick so the weakest point will be in the design."

"Because of human error," I stated.

"Exactly. That's how things improve in our industry because of design errors that aren't discovered until *after* the product has been released on the market. *So* if this was my MUM stick and it had all these programs on it, like tail minus *f*, and had the ability to check e-mails, then it's most likely your brother ran the stick as a portable web server. And if he did"—she typed "Self-extracting" and hit Enter—"Maybe by loading my own web server on the MUM stick with a preconfigured server it'll run websites and webapps directly from it. It's worth a try." She typed again and waited for the computer to respond. "By creating a portable server of my own, I can use a ZIP file and hopefully extract the files on Hunter's portable web server, which is a lot easier to execute than decrypting. It's also a long shot."

A window popped up on the screen and Carmen moved the mouse to a box labeled RUN. Before she clicked, she glanced at me. "There's also a very good chance your brother placed some kind of program on this that will self-destruct if I do the wrong thing."

I rubbed the stubble on my chin. "How far did Georgie get with the sixty-four bytes?"

She glanced at the screen on her iPhone. "Uh, sixteen. She decrypted sixteen bytes."

I slowly nodded. "Which leaves forty-eight bytes left to decrypt."

"Correct. And I don't mind doing that—there's still no guarantee we'll get them all decrypted or how long it'll take, but I'm in."

"I know." I stared at the MUM stick protruding from the computer. "This wouldn't have been the only place Hunter backed up his files. He'd have a copy on an online backup service. So, worst case, we have to find it, which—"

"Would be like having to find identical snowflakes," she said.

I grinned. "I was going to say like finding one specific clownfish in the entire ocean of sea life."

"Ah, a clownfish, a Nemo fan. I prefer Dory, but," she slowly exhaled, "same idea. If I end up erasing what's on the MUM stick, our only recourse will be to find the online backup service your brother used and try to access it." Lines burrowed across her forehead. I gently placed my hand on her wrist.

"Listen, I'm making the call. And I say go for it. If it ends up not working, we'll adjust. In the big scheme of things, it's not that big."

The softness in her eyes returned. "Si." She clicked RUN, and a string of code streamed across the screen.

"What does that mean?" I widened my eyes, but it didn't make the code any easier to decipher.

"It means I need to find a folder labeled Software and

install it on the control panel." She browsed a tree of folders that sprouted before her. After clicking on Software, she created a new folder and named it HUNTER.

"Okay, if I've done this correctly, then all the files will load into this file during the installation." She pointed to the button named Install.

"Once I hit Install, all the files should be extracted to the MUM stick." She pressed her thumb into the side of her head. "It could take a few minutes depending on the MUM stick's speed, although I doubt speed will be an issue. It's more of a"—she massaged her temple—"software issue. I'm worried what else Hunter loaded onto this."

"No stopping now," I said.

Carmen clicked on Install, and a window appeared.

Row upon row of extracting code streamed across the screen like a ticker-tape parade. Beneath the code, a bar labeled "Installation progress" appeared, with a green light that slowly inched its way across the bar.

"Ay Dios mio! I think it's working!"

I focused on the green light and waited until it completely filled the installation bar and shone like a glow worm. When it appeared as though the extraction process was finished, a window opened directing Carmen to finish the installation. This direction appeared as a question.

The first question asked if we wanted to add shortcuts to the start menu and desktop. Carmen entered *N*.

"We don't want to create start menu links, we just want to be able to access it," she said.

She reminded me of Hunter, who always explained even

the most obvious geek speak to me. I mean anyone who's ever downloaded Adobe Reader or iTunes knows what that means to access a download. But I did what I always did with my little brother and acted as if I were as computer clueless as they imagined. That didn't stop me from reading the questions that prompted us forward, and the next one made me laugh. Carmen looked at me and lifted her hands from the keyboard.

"What? Do you want me to stop?"

I shook my head. "No, it's another three-worded beauty, 'Should I proceed?'"

Her lips turned up in a wickedly sexy smile. "Well, should I?"

"Si," I said.

Her dimples shot across her face as she entered *Y*. I think we both held our breath and waited for the computer to respond. We waited.

And waited.

And waited some more.

"Uh, this may take a while." Her face scrunched. "Do you mind waiting?"

"*Not. At. All.*" I made sure my three little words had impact. I took her wrist and gently pulled her to me. Our lips met in a rushed embrace of energy that whirled around us like a cyclone. Whatever happened outside our funnel couldn't touch the force that swept us further and further into each other. Our lips became one as our bodies hungered for each other's touch.

I reached into her hair and lightly trailed my fingers

along her scalp like a breeze. Her back arched, and when she found her center again she nibbled on my earlobe, sending heat up my neck and into my cheeks. Her moans turned me inside out with sweet ecstasy.

I reached beneath her and scooped her up in my arms. She gasped.

"You're so strong."

"Carmen, you've got to weigh a buck twenty, wet."

She grinned. "Now, how'd you know I was wet?"

Despite myself I blushed, and Carmen leaned her head against my chest. "Oh, Hank." It again sounded like hunk.

I gently laid her on the floor before heading to the entrance to lock the door to the classroom, draw the protective shade and kill the overhead lights, which weren't bright and actually provided ambient, glare-free lighting. But I didn't want any lights—computer-friendly or otherwise to illuminate us. This was our time, but it did make me lightly chuckle. "All I need is a little Marvin Gaye up in here, and the mood is complete."

Her laughter was like a trigger to my cock. My body responded with an urge to hear her husky, sexy laugh in my ear while I buried myself deep inside her. I lay beside her; our hearts beat to a steady tempo of want, need, and desire.

I fingered the waistband of her slacks and knew I'd never master the button and zipper. I dipped my hand between her flat stomach and slacks.

"All this talk about banging," I said in her ear, "gave me a few ideas."

The air warmed between us, caught in the heavy rush of

surprise when my fingers found her wet with anticipation. She responded to me with raised hips, and her hands clawed my shoulders. Things were moving fast.

"Uh, we should probably stop. I don't have a condom."

But the rapid fire of my pulse and her heavy breathing disagreed. Neither of us could stop, nor did we want to. I wanted her, and from the warmth that released on my fingertips as I gently moved in and out of her, she wanted me too.

Her hands caressed my body with a passion that tingled my skin and awoke my senses. Her coconut scent intensified as her body heightened in pleasure. She unbuttoned my fly and slid off my jeans before I had a chance to stop the momentum.

"Are those Brazilian trunks?"

I raised an eyebrow. "Like 'em?"

"Mucho."

I glanced at the green-and-black-striped boxer-like trunks. "They're shorter, tighter, and don't ride up my thigh."

"And what thighs you have." Her blue eyes steadied on my legs, which thanks to soccer and football were probably my best feature. No chicken legs here.

"The men wear those Brazilian shorts on the telenovelas I watch with my abuelita, but they use them as swim trunks." She still hadn't made eye contact with me, her focus shifting to my bulge.

"These are the underwear version."

Her blue eyes flickered up to mine with delight. "Hank,

muy, muy caliente."

Carmen made me feel as hot as she said I was. I pulled off my jersey and the T-shirt beneath it, tossed them to the side, and gently moved my hand to the top of her pants, where I fumbled with the button.

"Let me." She unhooked her slacks and slid them off to reveal long, tapered, toned legs that wrapped around me.

I practically ripped apart her uniform shirt until it opened and a white sheer bra revealed dark areolas and miniature gumdrop-sized nipples. With her black hair brushing the top of her honeyed shoulders, long legs, toned stomach, full breasts, and silky wet patch, Carmen looked like a Playboy bunny, and I wanted to taste and delight in every inch of my private centerfold.

My hand returned to her clit. Her soft black hair wasn't shaved into a thin landing strip or completely bare. Carmen had a thick, full, though nicely groomed, bush that made my dick throb. I slowly pulled my trunks down, and my long, hard shaft rose between us.

"Muy grande," she said, with a saucy wink.

The girl was nothing but trouble, which drew me to her like a parched man to an oasis. If she wanted *grande*, I'd give it to her. I slid my hand down my cock, stroking it to its fullest. Then in one quick move, I flipped her onto her stomach, reached around, and cupped her breasts, lightly rubbing her nipple while her ass rose toward me. I gently bit the side of her neck while my finger lightly trailed her spine to the small dip that led to her round ass. I flicked my tongue across her ass, causing Carmen to quiver beneath me. She gave new meaning to the word petite. Her body was firm, compact, and fucking off-the-charts hot. She was a wonderland for my hands, which roamed across every curve and slender dip. The more my hands wandered, the more she moaned.

Her legs opened, and I placed my cock between her thighs, slowly dipping the tip against her warm clit. I slowly pulled back, trailing the head along her moist folds up to her tight ass that took every ounce of control not to bury myself into.

I repeatedly teased her clit while she groaned and begged me to end the foreplay.

"Hank, please."

"Please what?"

She glanced over her shoulder, her blue eyes sparking with intensity. "Please… me."

I reached above her, brought her wrists out in front of her, and held them together with one hand. She wanted pleasure, and I wanted to indulge her every wish. And the best way to gratify a woman with a body that was made for carnal delight was to delay gratification.

While I held her captive with one hand, my other hand gently flicked across her swollen clit. She writhed beneath me; her cries filled the space between us, and the heat we generated could charge a supercomputer.

There was only one thing standing in our way of decadent delight. I leaned toward her and whispered in her ear, "I *really* don't have a condom."

"It's *really* okay. I'm on the shot."

"Is that like the pill?"

"It's a birth control shot in my ass every three months, but…" She paused. "I mean the shot takes care of the getting pregnant part but not the, uh, you know."

"STDs. I'm clean, but I get it," I said.

Carmen looked toward the file cabinet. "I bet money there's condoms on one of those shelves. I've heard about after-exam parties that happen in here so I'm thinking if they stock red cups for their beer, they probably have everything else that's needed for a little fun."

I gently released her and walked to the file cabinet where I found an assortment of pens, pencils, and folders. I made my way through the shelves until I hit the bottom one. I rummaged behind a stack of CDs and spotted a box of condoms. *Nice.*

I grabbed one and returned to Carmen, who raised her willowy body toward me. I gripped the slender curve of her hip while I covered my cock with a condom. The tip of my cock slowly pushed past her wet clit and toward the moist lips that waited for me. I slid partially in and then out, never fully immersing myself inside her.

The sensation didn't just drive Carmen crazy, it drove me nuts. I mentally calculated how many condom boxes would equal a pallet, desperate to avoid losing my load prematurely. Carmen deserved a long, slow, sensual experience, even if I had to visualize fish guts on the loading dock in Newport, Oregon.

Carmen wasn't trying to lose herself anywhere but in the moment. She squirmed beneath me, trying to break free, trying to have use of her hands, but I leaned over her and whispered in her ear, "Not yet."

Her silky-smooth hair brushed against my cheek, and I buried my nose in her luxurious mane that smelled as exotic as she looked.

All senses were on overdrive. Carmen was a visual feast. Her siren cries reached into me and grabbed hold of my masculinity. She smelled like coconuts dripping with the musky scent of sex. Her skin felt like silk, and my desire to do right by her awakened a dormant part of my soul that had long given up on finding a woman like Carmen.

"Please, Hank, I want you."

To deny Carmen was impossible. I gently pushed into her, and it felt like breaking a seal.

She gasped, and again I spoke.

"I can stop."

She shook her head. "No. You're just bigger than I expected." She turned to make eye contact with me. "Don't. Stop. *Please*. Don't. Stop."

Every woman's warning, which usually broke the rhythm. Or at least my concentration. But this wasn't just any woman. This was Carmen. Her cries were directives. I wanted to please her more than myself. I deeply embedded myself into her, and moved with a tempo that didn't require me to pull in and out. Despite her protests, I didn't want to hurt her.

"Pleasure," I said with my dick throbbing inside her, "not pain."

My balls swung against her thighs as our momentum slowly built. The more she got used to me, the more she rocked our bodies together.

Carmen said something in Spanish that I didn't understand nor fully hear. But when her back arched, she tightened her hold around my cock, I knew she was close to release.

I kept the pace until a sudden gush of warmth flowed over my cock and oozed down my balls. To make a beautiful woman like Carmen orgasm was its own high. I increased my drive, released her wrists, and placed my hands on either side of her lean hips. I dug into her. I didn't even try to quell the beast; I dove deep to immerse my entire cock inside her. She met my desire with her own, and when I hit the spot that made my cock feel like it would explode, in turn I hit hers.

"Oh, God, oh, God!"

As Carmen came again, I thrust and bore down against her, unloading deep inside her. I was still coming when I leaned my head against her back, trying to regulate my breathing.

Her voice was all I heard. "Muy bien, muy, muy bien."

"Gracias," I said.

"De nada."

My head was still on her back when I felt her tense beneath me. I glanced up. "What's wrong?"

"I'm late."

"I realize we just had sex, but I don't think it happens that fast."

She giggled. "No! I'm late for *trabajo.*"

"Oh, work. Damn." Though I don't think my face or voice sold it. And the fact that I wasn't rushing to get off her probably didn't help.

"Yeah, I can tell you're heartbroken." She shook her head and wiggled out from beneath me.

I raised an eyebrow. "I wish I could say I was sorry…."

She giggled. "I bet."

I kissed the inside of her thigh before she totally moved away.

"Ah, Hank, tell me you're really a millionaire and we can sail away on your yacht."

"No yacht, but I've got a surfboard."

She smiled down at me. "I can surf."

"Of course you can." I kissed the tender skin along her thigh, inhaling her coconut-scented skin.

"I didn't say I was any good. Only that I can surf."

"I'm probably not much better, so we can paddle out together and catch a wave back to shore."

"How about if we just paddle away to Catalina?" she said.

"Or the Oregon Coast?" I kissed her again, tasting her skin, which was sweet like nectar. "I think you'd like Newport. It's nothing like the Newport you're familiar with. Newport, Oregon, has a small-town feel that never grows old."

She smiled, and I felt like Hunter's loss meant something more than just the tragedy attached to it.

She gently rolled away from me and began to dress. "I've got to call the hotel."

I quickly dressed, pulled out her chair beside the computer, and handed over her iPhone. She thumbed the screen awake and quickly scrolled through her contacts.

"We can come back tonight," I said, but she shook her head with her phone pressed against her ear. "Not now. If we stop the program at this point, we're guaranteed to lose everything that's on this stick for sure." She held up a finger that I tried to bite, and she giggled.

"Hey, Katie, it's Carm." She smiled. "*Buenas tardes* to you too. Hey, I'm here at the college banging with Hank."

I raised an eyebrow, and this Katie gal must have said something, because Carmen's face turned red.

"Banging code," she said. "We're *banging code*. Hank. No, Hank. H-a-n-k. He's Hunter's brother." She turned toward the colorless wall in the computer lab. "Si." She paused. "Muy bueno."

Oh, they're talking about me and so far it's good. Very good. Muy bueno *good.* I tapped Carmen on the shoulder. She turned, the question forming on her face.

"Tell her I may appear big and dumb, but I'm smarter than I look, and I don't look too bad."

Carmen's laughter was rich and warmed me from the inside out.

"Tell her you need to address the elephant in the room and that you're wearing peanut butter perfume," I said, making myself laugh.

Carmen couldn't seem to breathe from all her giggling.

I waved my hands like I was trying to flag down a plane, when really I just didn't want Carmen to stop laughing. It was the sweetest sound I never knew I missed. "No, no, tell her that you're dealing with a really big problem, and his name is Hank. Or Hunk, either works."

Carmen handed me the phone. "Here. She wants to talk to you."

I raised an eyebrow and held the phone against my chest. "Well, you've already introduced me to your family, and since you haven't been disowned for that, and you're still talking to me, meeting your friend should be a piece of cake. Which reminds me, should we get dessert after this?"

Carmen's eyes twinkled.

I moved the phone to my ear. It was still warm from Carmen's touch. "This is Hank."

"Hello, Hank, this is Katie Bogart." Her voice was nothing like Carmen's. It wasn't as smooth, honeyed, or soft. It wasn't a bad voice; it just wasn't a melody to my soul like Carmen's.

"Hello, Katie Bogart. How can I help you today?"

Carmen watched with rapt interest and I didn't want to disappoint, but I wasn't sure how manly I could be on a telephone call. Still, I tried. I crossed my legs and arched an eyebrow like I was the latest incarnation of Bond. James Bond.

"I was with Carmen when we went to your brother's room, and I just wanted you to know how hard she tried to save your brother's life. I've never witnessed such bravery." Katie paused, and I swallowed. "I was still in shock when he opened the door and suddenly passed out, but Carmen went right to him. She never left his side. Ever."

Tears streamed down my face quicker than I could wipe them away. I cleared my throat, but the damage was done.

Hunter didn't die alone. I knew he hadn't, but to hear it from someone else somehow made it real. I went from the suave and sophisticated superspy to a sobbing simpleton in a matter of seconds.

"Thank you" was all I knew to say. I handed the phone to Carmen.

"Hey," she said, and reached for my hand. "Are you okay?"

I nodded, wiping my face.

"Yeah, sorry, I'm here," she said. *"What did you say?"*

Carmen listened to Katie, but looked at me. Compassion filled her face.

"Oh, okay. I understand." She glanced at the clock. "So, can you cover for me with Richard? I'm training Mr. Harpington's nephew, Bryce. Oh, he left for the day? After a two-hour lunch? Really? Why? Oh." Her eyes widened and then she whispered, "We went from 90 percent occupied to forty so they let Bryce go home."

"Wow."

"I know." There was a long pause, and when Carmen spoke she looked directly at me. "Yeah, he's a special guy. Of course I will." There was an inflection in her voice, and I knew Carmen had just promised something. "If you can come up with some bullshit reason why I'm late from my very long, two-hour lunch like maybe you're having me pick something up from the printer? Yeah, that'd be great and that'll cover my tardiness with Dick. Thank you. I appreciate it. We shouldn't be much longer."

"What will you do?" I asked, trying to be playful again,

but the moment had passed. "You said, 'I will.' Will what?"

"I will be careful," she said.

"Careful? Careful with what? The computers?"

"Your heart," she said, and turned sideways in the chair, tucking her slender legs between mine. "Katie made me promise that I'd be careful with your heart."

I shrugged. "You don't have to be careful with me. I'm Hank the Tank. I'm fine."

She placed her hand on my thigh and pulled herself closer to me. "It's okay if you aren't. Even tanks break down."

I clenched my jaw, but this woman saw through me. "I know. I'll be okay. This was helping. Hacking and *banging* code with you." I smiled. "It was really helping, because for a few minutes I wasn't thinking about my brother. And when I did, it was with good memories." I spread my arms. "This is the best way for me to honor him."

"Okay." She leaned up and kissed my cheek. "Then let's go back to banging." A wry smile crossed her face and the loss that filled my heart was lightened, if only for a moment.

She held her finger above the Enter key while a string of directories automatically appeared, followed by commands for each directory.

"When the last file loads, I'll finalize the changes by pressing Enter," she said. Her face glowed in front of the screen. Finally, a final command appeared.

"Oh, damn, the moment of truth." She hit Enter.

The computer launched, and asked that we confirm that the current time zone was correct. Carmen did and then turned to me.

"That's it." Shock filled her face. "I think we can now run the files through the control panel, or we can exit and run the files from any other computer with this MUM stick. I mean, if you want to take it with you and try it out on your own."

"And miss this moment with you?" I shook my head. "No way, fancy pants. Like I said before, we're in this together. Hit Enter or whatever is needed to run the MUM stick files on your web server."

Carmen hit Enter and then opened the folder that appeared on the MUM stick. It launched another file. She clicked Start beside the file, and the webserver surfaced in a Windows environment. There was a lot I didn't recognize, but I knew Windows when I saw it. I worked with the program every day in the purchasing department. A message instantly surfaced. "Windows Firewall has blocked some features of the Apache HTTP on all public and private networks."

"What does that mean?" I asked. "Does it mean we can't access the files?"

She smiled. "No, it means you just have to give Apache access. The firewall popped up because the college has that programed to default on their system whenever an unknown device is loaded onto the system, but that means...."

"That the files extracted and are on this system?"

"*Si*. The files did extract and are *available* to open on this system."

"So, it worked?" I stared into her eyes. Carmen wasn't someone who needed or probably even liked being the center of attention. Her confidence was quiet, yet assured, bold, yet gentle. Her strength and independence stirred something inside of me that I'd thought was missing. "You did it."

She smiled so brightly I knew my brother was in the room with us. "It worked. And *we* did it."

Carmen stirred feelings that I'd thought I'd never experience. I'd envied the easy way my brother could be with women, while I was always clumsy and inept. But, for whatever reason, she made me feel confident and capable. Perhaps her inner strength enabled me to look beyond my outer self and see that I was much more than I appeared. Carmen had called me her hero, and when I was with her I felt like one.

CHAPTER **TWENTY-TWO**

I clicked the link to open the default administration page. "If everything works correctly, we should see a page in our browser that asks for our default language."

"Español, am I right?"

I shook my head. "Yeah, that's it. Let's make reading your brother's files more difficult by having them translated into Spanish."

"Uh, you mean Mexican, don't you?"

I frowned. "That guy was a jerk."

"I'm glad you see that now."

I shrugged. "Jerks are easy to spot. Bigotry isn't. It's not usually that blatant."

"Well, you shouldn't have to deal with any of it."

Hank made me feel protected in a way that wasn't possessive, and desired in a way I'd never known. When I was with Hank, I felt complete. An orange window popped up, along with a message that made my heart skip a beat.

Congratulations! You have successfully installed

Xammarple on this system! Now you can start using Apache. You should first try >Status< on the left navigation to make sure everything works fine.

"Okay." I slowly exhaled. "One last step." I clicked the Status link on the left sidebar to make sure everything was running correctly. Another orange box surfaced, with a directory of files that brought tears to my eyes.

"Are those Hunter's files?" The shock in his voice matched the amazement I felt.

"They sure are."

A message above the file directory noted: *This page offers you one page to view all the files and information about what's running and working and what isn't.*

I quickly scanned the Status column beside each exported file, and a green Activated light appeared beside seven of the nine files. A red light that read Deactivated appeared beside two files.

"What does that mean?" Hank pointed to the red status boxes.

"It means two of your brother's files extracted, but he must have loaded an extra level of encryption on them, and it looks like he also added a data disaster system recovery program to prevent them from opening in our web server."

"Data disaster system? What's that again?"

"It's basically a safety net for removable and network drives. If he ever accidentally deleted something, he'd be able to recover the deleted data without installing more software, which runs the risk of overwriting any remaining files. Shit." I scratched the side of my head. "I'm learning more from hacking his MUM stick than I have in four years at college."

He smiled. "Hunter wanted to teach, but he never got his undergraduate degree, so colleges wouldn't even consider him for their IT program."

"That's bullshit. Experience is the best teacher, and your brother had a PhD in coding."

"What do you think's on those two deactivated files?"

I pursed my lips. "I'm not sure. But they were important enough that he safeguarded them. However...." I directed the mouse to the green-lit files and hit Open on each link. "There's seven files we can access, so that's something."

"Girl, that's more than something, that's fucking brilliant."

Happiness surged through me. "It'll take a while until they download, but the good news is that they *are* downloading."

"Why would Hunter only protect two of the nine files?"

I pointed toward the MUM stick on the side of the computer. "One of the biggest drawbacks to a thumb drive or MUM stick is that they're so *pequeña*. Small. They're *way* too easy to lose, which is probably why your brother put it on a lanyard around his neck. But imagine if he lost this? Any sensitive information on the stick, which he wanted to keep private, would be available to anyone—unless he secured it. Granted, he encrypted it, but it looks like he also added a 'beat the spies' program to prevent hacking of these two files."

"So why didn't Georgina hack it? I mean the MUM stick."

I raised my eyebrows. "She was on a monitored work computer. Georgina's good because she's cautious. She wasn't going to try anything with the MUM stick that could be traced or monitored. Until you mentioned hacking, I looked at this encrypted MUM stick as something to decrypt. I never considered hacking it by tricking the MUM stick to think our web server was a duplicate drive on his stick."

"It's brilliant."

I rolled my eyes. "It was luck."

"No, it's talent. I watched my brother for years, and you have many similar qualities. It's like you just know how to talk to the computer."

I laughed. "Thanks. You're one of the few people who truly appreciate computer geeks. I think when most people think of a computer programmer or developer, they think of a nerd in a basement with a case of Mountain Dew and Cheetos, banging out computer code."

"There you go again with that banging."

I felt my cheeks flush. "Ha. Ha. It's computer slang. And if I *really* wanted to bore or possibly impress you, I'd rattle on about keyboard slang."

Hank leaned his elbows on his knees, bridging the little space between us. "Go ahead, bore me."

He had strong features that matched his physique, which was a good thing. If he'd had a boyish face with such a burly body, it would have been like dating Baby Huey. I glanced at his lips, which were ripe for nibbling, and then to his eyes, which swirled in color like they were ready to reveal something.

"All right, I'll let you in on my favorite keyboard slang."

His greenish-brown eyes favored green. "Let me in."

I raised an eyebrow. "I already did, Oregon. Besides, computers aren't meant to be sexy."

"No, but certain programmers are."

Hank took the art of flirting to the deeper end of the pool. Fortunately, he was tall enough to not be in over his head.

"Back to geeky computer jargon." I tried to act serious, when my body wanted to play some more with Hank's tank. "So, if you've ever hit or beaten a piñata or, perhaps sipped a piña colada, you're familiar with the Spanish *tilde*. But in keyboard computer slang, the *tilde* is known as a twiddle or squiggle."

"A twiddle, huh? I thought that was just something you did with your thumbs when you're bored."

"No!" I swatted his shoulder and giggled. "When computer geeks are writing those long pages of HTML code, they have shortcut names for commands on the keyboard. Seriously." I gripped his shoulder and felt nothing but muscle. "I could put you to sleep with all the slang, but that's not what we're here to do." I glanced at the computer that was still in the process of downloading Hunter's files.

"Ah, come on, one more."

I rapped my fingers on the desk. "Okay, but let's mix it up."

"Mix away, minx."

"What sign has been called a monkey tail, a meow, and some geeks call it a strudel?"

"Monkey tail, meow, and strudel...." Hank tapped his chin with his forefinger. "Hmm." He playfully leaned against me to glance at the keyboard. But then his focus shifted, his posture straightened, and the intensity in his eyes was hard to read. Hank didn't appear to be someone who liked to lose. He was a competitor, and my keyboard challenge tested his sportsmanship. Soon it would be time to see if he was a gracious winner or an obnoxious one. I wasn't a fan of the latter.

"Hmm...." He tilted his head, as if the keyboard would look different sideways.

I clenched my jaw. *Please don't be a sore loser. Handle defeat with ease.* I was attracted to strong men, but not men with powerfully poor attitudes.

Suddenly, Hank's face lit with surprise. "Oh! There it is." He paused. "It's the 'at' sign?" Uncertainty filled his masculine voice. "Is that right?"

"Si. Muy bien."

"Really? I got it right?" He squinted at the top row of numbers and the signs above them.

Ah, he's not just a gracious winner, he's almost a reluctant one. He was the kind of guy who would genuinely feel badly for me if I ever lost at his expense. *Nice.*

"The 'at' sign does look like a monkey tail, and I see the strudel. But a meow?"

I tilted my head. "It's a sleeping cat."

"Oh, that's cute." He high-fived me. "To monkey tails, meows, and strudel."

Our hands slapped against each other's and his win felt

like mine. Heat radiated through my body, and the computer between us seemed to respond. File folders began to explode onto the screen.

"Here we go. The moment we've been waiting for." I clicked on the first of the seven files that were labeled by a string of numbers that I couldn't decipher. They weren't dates. *Maybe file stamps?*

The first file opened in Excel to reveal a spreadsheet. Columns and rows with names and numbers filled the document page. "It looks like a time sheet, but that can't be right."

Hank tipped the screen toward him. "It's not a time sheet, it's a profit and loss statement."

"Why would your brother save this?"

He held a finger toward me, and I grabbed it. "Don't point."

"I'm not." He grinned and flipped his wrist, seizing my hand in a matter of seconds. He held on to me—tight, like he had when he was inside me. My body flushed.

"Hold up. Give me a second." His focus narrowed on the computer screen. "Can we print this?"

"We should be able to. But let me check." I attempted to pull away, but he was too strong. His hold on me tightened.

"Where you going?"

I smiled. "The printer's in the corner. I've got to make sure it's loaded with paper, turned on, and ready to print."

"Right." He removed his hand, which was like a vise that totally turned me on.

I jumped up, headed toward the printer, and gave a

thumbs-up. Hank moved the mouse, and within minutes the printer spit three legal-sized sheets onto the tray. I brought them to him.

"So, profit and loss from the Waterfront?"

He slowly shook his head. "No. From the Newport Heights."

"Qué?"

"These are profit and loss statements from the Newport Heights."

"How can you tell?"

Hank pointed to the footer on the bottom of the page. "It says so right here."

I lightly whacked him. "I didn't see that."

"It'd be easy to miss unless you read these as religiously as I do."

"What is it that you do?"

"I run the purchasing department at the Carlyle Hotel in Newport, Oregon."

His response sounded rehearsed—there was no emotion or thrill attached to it.

"So, you're the Director of Purchasing?"

He nodded.

"Wow. That's great."

He grimaced. "Not so much, but I work with my buddies from high school and college, so that's cool."

While he studied the spreadsheet, I studied him. His build was easily the first thing someone noticed about Hank. But beneath the brawn, there was a beauty that revealed itself through his emotions and actions. Clearly not for his job, but his family, friends, and with me, Hank's passion was as deep as the ocean.

"This is going to take some time to decipher. Can you print the other files my brother saved?"

I nodded. "Absolutely." I right-clicked on each file and sent the documents to the printer. The corner of the room hummed with the rustling of paper that filled the tray in a hodgepodge order.

"I'm starving." Hank glanced around the room and set his sights on the instructor's desk. He pulled open each drawer, mumbling as he rummaged through the contents. "There's got to be…." He shut the drawers. "This is a college, right?"

I grabbed the papers from the printer and shuffled them together. "That's right."

"Where the hell is a file folder?"

I laughed. "I thought you were looking for food."

"No, a file folder."

"Uh, it's a computer classroom. The only file folders are on the PCs and Macs."

His face fell. "Good point."

"But in the file cabinet behind you, I think they keep interoffice envelopes. They're not much to look at, but they'll do the trick."

"Smart thinking, fancy pants."

I grinned, returned to the computer to close the files, and shut down. But before I did, I glanced at Hank. While his back was to me, I quickly opened the college e-mail program, attached each of his brother's files, including the two deactivated ones, and sent them to myself. I don't know what possessed me to do it, only that I did, and then I didn't do anything to stop the mayhem. Worse, the message took longer to load than I'd expected. *Come on. Come on. Come on.*

"You'd think they'd organize this mess," Hank said behind me.

"Computer nerds." I tapped my foot. *Shit. Come on. Send.* When the Send button finally disappeared, the message flew off the screen like a heat-seeking missile, and I could only hope my e-mail would be as effective in hitting the target of my home e-mail inbox.

"Found one!" Hank returned to me just as I closed the e-mail program, safely removed the MUM stick, and shut down the computer that was normally left on all day. But I didn't want the next IT'er to search our history or even attempt to access what we did. Heat inched up my neck and into my cheeks. *What did I do?* I handed the stick to him and brushed my hands against my slacks like I was getting rid of dust, when in reality the sweat of guilt covered my palms. Angst turned me inside out, but all I said was, "So, food? Mexican, Chinese, subs?"

"You had me at food."

I nervously smiled. *Why take his brother's files without asking?* I tried to understand my rash action, and only one word surfaced. Trust. *What the hell, Carmen? If not Hank, then who?*

"Carm, you okay?"

I nodded. "Just hungry.

"Then let's blow this taco stand and go to a real one."

My feet were heavy, and a knot twisted my stomach. *Delete it.* "Hey, can I check my e-mail first? Before we leave."

"Sure. Is there a men's room?"

I hiked my thumb behind me. "Outside, just down the hall."

As soon as the door shut behind Hank, I logged on to the college computer, clicked open the e-mail, and looked for the message with the attached files. *Delete. Delete. Delete.* But it wasn't there. *What the hell?*

I clicked into the Sent folder, and the last message I sent from my campus e-mail was to Brenda in the IT department about artwork for the graduation announcements. *That was two days ago.* I hit the refresh button and my Sent folder updated. *Okay, that's better.*

The e-mail with the nine attachments was on top. I breathed a sigh of relief and was about to delete it when I leaned toward the screen.

"No, no, no, no." I held my face in my hands, but nothing could change my fuckup. "I sent it to my e-mail at the hotel? *What?*"

"What's that?" Hank had the soft-footed grace of a ballet dancer. He had silently crossed the room like he was auditioning for the title role in *The Nutcracker*. And he wasn't even trying to be stealthy. With just his normal gait, Hank could sneak up on a cat and scare half the feline's lives away.

I closed the e-mail program, hit the bottom settings button to close the computer, and turned toward him. "Oh,

I meant to send something to my home e-mail or even my college inbox, but looks like I sent it to work."

"Can't you access your work e-mail from here?"

I shook my head. "Nope. They block us from accessing our e-mail off-site as part of the updated security protocols."

"Well, I have to swing by the hotel to get Hunter's things. You can change out of your uniform, log on, and forward the e-mail to your home."

His kindness only made my stupidity and impulsiveness feel more like a horrible, awful, mean betrayal. He stared at me.

"Sorry, yeah," I said. "That's a great idea. But what about lunch? Or a late lunch?"

"Lunch will be an early dinner at my hotel."

My heart went from beating fast to a dead stop. "Your hotel?"

"Did you forget the hotel key we found? We still don't know what room it belongs to, but with your help, we will. You game?"

"Absolutely." If there were any way I could remedy this, I would—and hopefully before Hank ever knew.

CHAPTER **TWENTY-THREE**

"So how drunk do you think I'll have to get him? You know, to tell him about copying the files? Or maybe I don't say anything."

Katie's brown eyes widened. "Uh, who are you and what did you do with my levelheaded, even-keeled colleague and friend?"

"She's *hasta luego*."

Katie leaned forward in her chair. "And when did this departure happen exactly?" I didn't think the woman ever left her office. It's where I always found her, and despite how busy she was, she was always available for me.

"Well, we had sex, and afterward things were going well."

Katie about shot out of her seat. "What? You had sex with him?"

"Why don't you just issue a memo or get on the loudspeaker? I don't think the girls in the cafeteria heard."

Katie leaned forward and lowered her voice. "Carmen?

You had sex with Hank."

I nodded. "I did."

"And?" Her brown eyes widened with interest.

"And it was unbelievable. Ah-mazing, and pretty much the best two orgasms of my life."

"Two? He gave you two orgasms? On the first try?" She paused. "Or was it multiple tries?"

I slowly shook my head. "Nope, on the first time. Hank the Tank is aptly named. The man's a beast."

"Wow." Katie leaned back. "I guess so." She tilted her head. "Then what happened?"

"Well, after having sex with a relative stranger in the college computer lab, my moral decline sank further when I copied his brother's files and sent them to myself as a backup."

"Moral decline?" She shook her head. "Nah. I mean, you don't *really* feel badly about hooking up with Hank?"

I smiled. "No. It's probably just Catholic guilt."

"Well, hell, that can be remedied Saturday at confession."

We both laughed.

"Okay, so back to your computer file mishap. You panicked. And you panicked because…."

Instinctively I crossed my arms in front of my chest. "I didn't panic."

Her mouth opened as if to counter, and then closed.

"I didn't."

She nodded.

"I didn't panic. I copied the files, and that's that. I mean, I'm as all-in with Hank as a girl can be. I barely know him, but I'm in. And I like being in. But this scheme to uncover what his brother was working on? What is that really? We don't know. It's probably nothing." I uncrossed my arms and opened my hands, palms up. "So, we spend his last days left in California working on something that could lead to nothing, and then what happens?" I flung out my arms. "He returns to Oregon, and I return to being alone. *That's* what happens."

Katie's face softened. "Oh, Carm, you like him. It wasn't just sex. You *really* like him."

I blew out a mouthful of air. "He's a nice guy. And a *really* good sport, who has the most perfect body I've seen on a man. Of course I like him, but what does that matter? He lives in Oregon, and I live in California. So, I can like him, but I can't *like-like* him."

"Sure. Just like I tried not to *like-like* Chris Bogart."

"That was different. You made a complete mess of things when you made out with TJ."

She slightly smiled. "That's true. When I acted impulsively, I sabotaged the budding attraction Chris and I had for each other. My actions were hasty, irresponsible, and reckless. I'm sure you're not familiar with such thoughtless, careless behavior."

I sank in the chair opposite her desk. "So why did you do it?"

"Many reasons. I *was* attracted to TJ, but I think beneath that attraction there was a greater emotion dictating my actions, which was fear."

"Fear?"

"Sure. I was afraid. And that came out sideways. Bogart and I hadn't committed our feelings to each other, but that doesn't mean they weren't there. I hadn't gone *all-in* but we got close."

"So… what changed?" I asked even though I knew their story as well as I knew my own.

"It took breaking Bogart's trust for me to get over my trust issue."

"Trust, huh?"

Katie's magnetic smile warmed me when I felt so cold inside.

"That thought came to me. Like I don't trust Hank, but why?" I shrugged. "There's no reason not to trust him. I have *no* idea why I copied the files and sent them to myself. It's like you making out with TJ and Bogart finding out. I may have totally screwed things up with Hank."

"Not necessarily. Hank doesn't know you copied the files, right?"

I nodded. "Yeah. That's why I'm here. To erase what I did."

Katie smiled. "Then let's do that." She turned her computer monitor around and handed me the keyboard. "Hank doesn't know, and maybe later you can explain it to him. But for now, log on, delete, and move on."

"I hope to hell it's that easy."

CHAPTER **TWENTY-FOUR**

The guy reminded me of a David Bowie lyric. Though out of respect to the thin, white duke, I mentally tweaked the verse. When I stood in front of Michael Harpington, I heard a new melody to "The Jean Genie." The guy resembled a prince, but winked like a cad. His secretary, Hannah, didn't seem to mind. Her teeth were as white as her white-blonde hair when she smiled in his direction.

"Hannah-Banana, thanks for holding down the fort while I was gone." He eyed her from head to toe like she was ripe for the picking.

Harpington wasn't much of a man, but there was no point telling Hannah. She'd learn soon enough. Or she'd never learn. Some people refused to see others for who they really were; instead, they believed that the person would change for the better or, at the least, not get any worse over time. In either case, Hannah would be sorely disappointed when Michael Harpington proved to be no better than his shiny appearance.

I mean, what the fuck? His wardrobe probably cost more than my car, but all I could focus on was his oddly sunbaked skin. From the cuffs and collar of his tailored shirt, I was exposed to what could best be described as a pair of orange-colored hands and equally toned pencil neck. He definitely made a lasting impression. Not a really good impression, but a lasting one nonetheless.

"Hank, thank you for returning to the Waterfront."

I dwarfed his hand when we shook. "Not a problem."

I felt like I was having a flashback to when we played Oregon State. No matter how many times I blinked, I kept seeing the OSU mascot, an orange beaver. All Harpington needed was a pair of buck teeth and he'd be leading the Beaver faithful in cheer.

"How are your rooms at the Newport Heights?"

"Very nice, thanks." *Nothing like thanking a scumbag douche.*

He motioned toward the overstuffed black leather seat. I sank into the filling that would normally shrink someone when they sat across from the owner and founder of the Point Resort, whose executive chair was raised to elevate him. But I wasn't someone who shrank. *Asshole.*

"Hannah has a box organized with your brother's belongings that she left with Security, though"—he grimaced—"I have to say there wasn't much in his hotel room."

"Really?" I played along on his fishing expedition.

"Yes, it was troublesome to us as well. We didn't find any luggage, and his laptop was damaged in the… um…."

He brushed the back of his head and looked at me, as if Hunter's death was something he expected me to discuss.

I raised an eyebrow. *If you think I'm going to make this easier for you, you've got another think coming, buddy.*

"Well, during the staff's attempts to revive him." A look of fear flashed through his dark eyes.

Uh-oh. Now you did it. You actually mentioned the hotel's involvement.

"Actually, when he died," Harpington quickly corrected himself. "Hunter died." He cleared his throat as if the mere mention of my brother's death were hard to swallow, much like the hotel's chicken wings.

"Of course, the staff and management of the Waterfront Point would like to send flowers and make a donation in your brother's name to his favorite charity, or an organization, on his behalf. Perhaps you could direct us on that?" He reached into the top drawer of his mahogany desk and retrieved a checkbook ledger that he placed on the desk.

For real? Did this puke think he could just write a check and make it all go away?

Harpington uncapped his gold-accented pen and thumbed in the register to a blank check.

"The library."

"Excuse me?" He cocked his head so his ear pointed toward me.

"The library. I'm sure Huntington Beach has a library, if not a few."

"Well, yes, yes, there's the central library, and the Banning Branch on Banning Avenue." He lowered his voice.

"It's rather old and small."

"Perfect. The Waterfront can donate a new computer to the Banning Branch library."

"A computer?" His eyes widened. "Uh, well...."

I gave him a cold, hard stare. "Providing an older, smaller library with an up-to-date computer for the community is the best way to honor my brother."

"Yes, yes, of course. I'll have the IT department order a top-of-the-line computer." He capped his pen and steepled his fingers. "Speaking of computers. Your brother's laptop was, as I mentioned, damaged. However, our IT department tells me they could most likely repair and recover whatever files he may have been working on."

"No, that won't be necessary."

He slowly nodded.

"Before I forget." I shifted gears. "The two women who were with Hunter. My folks were hoping to get their names and addresses. How are they?" I asked, even though I had spoken to Katie, and I knew from being with Carmen that what they experienced wasn't something they were likely to forget anytime soon. Having Carmen's address would allow me to send her flowers. Or maybe balloons. Both? Too much?

"We can't give out staff members' addresses since it's a breach of privacy, but perhaps we could get the full spelling of their names and departments then your parents can send it directly to the hotel." Harpington tilted his head toward the office door, which remained open. "Hannah, could you confirm the spelling for Katie Bogart and Carmen Gonzalez's names and get their positions and departments from HR?" He returned his focus to me. "As to your question, Katie and Carmen seem to be doing fine. They were given four days off with pay to attend to their business."

He sounded as rehearsed and rote as an employee manual on how to handle bereavement.

"Four days?" I rubbed my chin. "That's such a short period of time to handle grief and then return to where it happened." Before Harpington could counter, I continued, "Our culture really doesn't deal well with grief. We expect people to come back and get on with things, and that's just not always realistic." I didn't know if I was lecturing him or myself. In the five stages of grief, I was either in denial, or I had jumped to the acceptance phase.

Hannah popped her head into the office. "Mr. Harpington, when I called HR they said that Security wants to see Carmen and that you'd know what it was about. Do you still want her department and such?"

"Uh, yes, please. Thank you." For a moment, his chiseled orange face appeared to crumple.

"Is everything okay with Carmen?" It felt like my heart had stopped.

Harpington took a moment and stared at me.

I didn't fill in the space with idle chatter. I waited. And I'd continue to wait until he told me what the hell Security wanted with Carmen.

Carmen was an answer to my prayers, and just down the coast. I probably should have been more specific in my prayers, since the Pacific coastline runs for hundreds of miles, which left this beauty about a thousand miles too far down that coast. But while we were on the same coast, I would protect her at all costs.

"Actually, things aren't okay with Ms. Gonzalez. It appears as though she accessed files that belonged to your brother."

I swallowed hard and tried to regulate my breathing. *How the hell did Harpington find out?* My face must have conveyed confusion, because Harpington was more than eager to make sense of my internal chaos.

"About thirty minutes ago, the IT department notified me that Ms. Gonzalez received an e-mail from an outside IP address with attachments that appear to belong to your brother."

What? "Aaaa.… Outside e-mail from mmmm… my brother?" My shock was as stammered as my speech. "Were you able to open the attachments?"

"Well, no. They were encrypted."

I slowly nodded. "But you believe they belonged to my brother?"

"The files were saved and named with a time stamp followed by, uh, a specific IP address. The files could only have been created by your brother when he was at the hotel."

"How do you know this?"

"We provided Hunter with his own IP address to work from while he was here at the hotel. So, whatever name he gave a file, it would follow with a date stamp and our IP address. And it's that IP address that appears on each file."

What a sleaze. No wonder my brother wanted to keep

eyes on you. "Okay. So why did Carmen have these files?"

"That's exactly what we intend to find out when we bring her into the security office for an interview. At the least, she's suspended, and at the most, her employment will be terminated. We don't take computer crime lightly."

"Crime?"

"The theft of financial information."

"How do you know she stole financial information if you couldn't open the files?" I looked at Harpington in feigned disbelief. He had no clue that I knew the contents of at least one file, which was a profit and loss financial spreadsheet for their biggest competitor, the Newport Heights. The other files were in Hunter's rental car, stuffed in an internal college mail envelope.

"Well, the, uh, file names identified the user."

I tilted my head. "Yah, I got that. You were able to identify them as Hunter's files by the time stamp and his own personal hotel-provided IP address that appeared beside whatever he named the files. But what I don't get is how you could tell from an IP address and time stamp that the files contained financial information." *What am I missing here?*

"It's difficult to explain," he said as a way of bypassing the conversation and his involvement, which was most likely rife with misconduct.

That's fine, asshole. Now that I know the files are time-stamped with a special IP address, I can sort them by time and fill in the missing puzzle chunks. What wasn't as simple to piece together was why Carmen e-mailed the files to herself. *Why would she do that?* I felt sick. *Is that why she wanted to check her e-mail at the college? Has she been playing me this entire time? She couldn't—could she?*

"Mr. Harpington, here's the names of the staff members who were there with your brother and the hotel's address. We can forward whatever your parents may want to send." Hannah handed him a slip of pink paper that he then handed to me, which I tucked into my jeans pocket.

"Oh," she said before leaving. "I almost forgot. Security called, and they have Carmen in their office. They're just waiting for you."

He politely grinned. He might have realized that Hannah-Banana was easy on the eyes, but empty between the ears.

"I hate to ask you to return once more to the hotel."

Then don't.

"However, I feel I should attend this meeting, especially since it concerns your brother. We're just asking questions at this point, nothing more or less, but I think my presence would be...." He paused as if considering his title and rank. "Well, significant." He began to rise from his elevated perch and I stood.

"I understand," I said, eye to eye with him. "And the best way to avoid a third trip to the hotel where my brother died is to accompany you to the Security office. Since," I placed my hands on my hips and took a broad stance in front of him, "you mentioned that this matter concerns my brother, I'd like to hear for myself how Carmen accessed those files. And why she e-mailed them and how."

If shock had a look, Harpington wore it. "Uh… well, that

may be an issue with Human Resources."

I raised an eyebrow. "Really? But you're just asking questions at this point—nothing more or less." My hands came off my hips with open palms, as if I had no ulterior motive than to help. "This is perfect, actually. I can gather Hunter's belongings and his laptop while I'm there." I forced a smile. "And if you find out what Carmen does or doesn't know, it may bring final closure to this for my folks. I'm told you have some papers you'd like them to consider signing."

"Yes, uh, just some forms to finalize the insurance claim for your parents."

I nodded. "I'd be happy to pass it along to our family attorney to review." I clapped my hands together. "So, I guess I'll follow you to the Security office, and then you can give me that paperwork."

"Certainly." Harpington took a long stride toward the door. "Actually, we could forward the form to your attorney for you. And save you that time."

"Nah." I waved away his suggestion with the evasive tactic that accompanied it. "I'll bring it to my folks tonight. I'm sure they'd like to read it first." *Or when I see them again in Oregon.* After cremating their son, they texted me that they took my brother home with them on the first flight out of Orange County to Eugene. They were probably driving from the airport to Newport right now. I opted to stay because there were too many things that didn't line up. And just like in football, when things don't line up, it's either an illegal formation or too many players on the field, and Carmen may just be the reason for the latter.

"Of course, of course. As a parent, I'd want to read the form as well."

I followed Harpington out of his office and made sure he heard my footfalls closing in on him.

CHAPTER **TWENTY-FIVE**

Carmen held her hands in her lap. Her face was flushed, and when she saw me a tear slipped down her cheek.

Oh, Carm. Why?

"Ms. Gonzalez," Harpington began, "this is Mr. Hank Hughes. He's Hunter Hughes's brother."

She stood and extended her hand. "Hi. I'm Carmen."

When our hands touched, something broke inside me. *Why? Doesn't she trust me? I trusted her.*

"Mr. Hughes asked to be part of this informal review, as it concerns his brother. Are you all right with that?" Harpington asked.

I expected to hear the lyrical way she said "Si," but instead she spoke English. "Yes."

"Excellent. We also have Sid from IT joining us." He nodded toward a gangly guy no older than my kid brother. "Sid and Hannah packed your brother's belongings."

Sid nodded toward a file cabinet behind the door. A box labeled Hunter Hughes made my chest ache.

"Okay, let's begin." Harpington commandeered the chair at the head of the small table in the corner of the Security office. He shifted his chair to allow Sid to sit beside him. Carmen was directed to the chair on the opposite end of the table, which left me in the middle.

Great.

Harpington glanced at the man in a security uniform. "Bill, will you give us the room?"

"Absolutely." He closed the door behind us.

I wasn't normally claustrophobic but the Security office tested my capacity for small, enclosed spaces.

Harpington didn't make eye contact with Carmen. His focus was on the file Sid presented him. "Carmen, could you tell us how it is that you came into possession of Mr. Hughes's computer files." He skimmed through the papers when Carmen shook her head.

"No."

This prompted Harpington's head to shoot up. "Excuse me?"

"I said, 'no.'"

"So, am I to understand that you won't tell us how you got Mr. Hughes's files, or is it that you don't know?"

"I know how they came into my possession."

"But you're choosing not to tell us?"

She slowly nodded. "That's correct."

Harpington leaned against the metal-framed chair and scratched the back of his head. "Do you understand the seriousness of this?" He glanced at Sid. "Should we get Janet from Human Resources to translate? Maybe there's no *comprende*."

My heart rate spiked. "Are you kidding me?"

Harpington and his skinny computer sidekick stared at me like I was about to get physical and they were about to wet themselves.

"Her English is perfect. She understands your question, she's just choosing not to answer," I said. My words were more effective than my muscles, and got the point across without them having to change their pants.

Still, Harpington gave his best scowl in my direction before shifting his glare to someone it may actually have an impact on—Carmen. "Is that true, Ms. Gonzalez? You understand what I'm asking."

"Yes, I understand."

"Yet you're unwilling to tell us how you came into contact with these files?"

"That's correct."

Harpington rapped his long, spindly fingers across the table. "And why is that? If you realize the severity of your actions, why not help yourself?"

"I realize that my employer reads my private e-mails without my consent," she said, and despite how mad I was I couldn't help but internally smile.

"I own every single computer in this hotel and run the network—that entitles me to look at whatever I want on *any* computer, including e-mails." Harpington narrowed his eyes. "The e-mail in question was *not* from a private account, it was on your employee e-mail server, which does not have the same expectation of privacy as a private e-mail, as per the hiring contract you signed when you were hired by the Waterfront."

Fucker. It wouldn't have mattered if Carmen received the e-mail etched in stone and involving a burning bush, Harpington would still claim jurisdiction because in his mind, he was the Almighty and the hotel was his kingdom.

"Yes, but computer hacking laws provide protection against viewing personal e-mails without consent," she said.

"Maybe you don't understand. As I stated, this e-mail was *not* on a personal, password-protected private e-mail. It was an employee e-mail," he said.

Sid, the spineless wonder, sat mute beside Harpington.

"You sent an e-mail to yourself on an employer-owned computer. That makes it visible for monitoring. And we do this monitoring, why?" Harpington didn't even wait for her or anyone to answer. "To ensure the anonymity and privacy of our guests. The Waterfront caters to the Hollywood and Washington elite that visit our property. We can't afford to have even one guest's stay compromised—by anyone."

"I didn't use the hotel computer," she said, and then looked at me. "I sent the e-mail and attachments from a computer on campus."

It felt like my heart shattered, and what was left fell to my stomach. *Why? Why would you do that?*

But before she could answer, Harpington's fist hit the table, and his jaw tightened. "The end result remains the same. The e-mail was received on an employer-owned computer, which makes it visible to our IT department. And in turn, me."

"Understood. I never should have sent myself the e-mail," she glanced at me. "I wasn't thinking, and I'm so sorry. I know that doesn't erase what I've done."

"Yet you tried to erase it," Sid said, finally speaking.

Carmen's eyes turned a cold shade of blue.

"Did you?" I leaned toward Carmen, blocking her stare down with Harpington and Sid. "Did you try to erase the e-mail?"

"I never meant to send it to begin with."

But you did. The truth slapped me in the face.

"Mr. Harpington, you've read my e-mail, which was blank. And it's obvious that Sid couldn't access the attached files, because if he could we wouldn't be here. I'm not going to tell you how or where I got the attachments. So, you can keep barraging me with questions without the benefit of a Human Resources representative, which I'm sure the local newspapers would eat up after the recent staged walkout for unequal employee treatment. Or you could let me go home."

"Or I could fire you right now," Harpington said in a voice that chilled the air and hit my last nerve.

That's it.

"I'm done listening to you both volley insults and insinuations back and forth. This isn't some Mexican standoff where you threaten each other." I looked from Harpington to Carmen. "This is about my brother. Hunter died in this hotel, and whatever he was working on is none of your damn business." I glared at Harpington, and then turned to Carmen. "Nor is it any longer your concern."

Sadness filled her face and tears spilled down her cheeks. It hurt to see her in pain, but enough was enough. Whatever I'd thought I had with Carmen, I clearly didn't. The only thing I could do was move on.

I pointed at Sid. "I want the e-mail and all the attachments deleted from the server—tonight."

I pushed out my chair and stood. "When the e-mail is deleted from the server, my family will sign whatever paperwork you have. In the meantime, I'm taking my brother's laptop and all his belongings. All I need now is proof that the e-mail was deleted by way of a written, signed, notified acknowledgement by you," I pointed to Harpington, "that Hunter's e-mail is no longer on your server or anywhere that you can access it on your hotel system. I want this letter delivered to me tonight at the Newport Heights. You both equally helped and hurt my brother in different ways, and I'm no longer going to be party to this. If either of you," I kept my finger pointed toward Harpington, and then shot it at Carmen, "continue this quest into my brother's work, I will legally hold you both accountable in court for his death."

I didn't bother to wait for either of them to defend themselves. There was no defense. And no way to bring back the one person who seemed to have been lost in all of this. None of this would bring Hunter home. I pushed the chair into the table, grabbed the box off the file cabinet, opened the door, and walked away. It was time for me to finally say goodbye and return to Oregon.

CHAPTER **TWENTY-SIX**

Rain streaked the broken windshield in my truck. A cold north wind blew off the Pacific that seeped through the window in my cab. I cranked the heat to high, but it did little to warm the chill that had settled in my skin.

What have I done?

I drove out of the employee parking lot and headed south toward Newport Beach. Pacific Coast Highway was slick from oil that the rain unearthed, yet cars sped past me. I stayed in the slow lane, not knowing where I was headed, only that I wasn't ready to go home. When I arrived at the front drive to the Newport Heights, I left the keys in my truck, grabbed my backpack, and headed toward the front desk.

"Hello!" I said as cheerfully as I could muster to the front desk clerk. "I'm looking for a guest that's staying here."

Her name tag read Taylor, and after she eyed my jeans and tank top from head to toe, she glanced over my head when she spoke, as if she were directing her comments to someone behind me who was perhaps dressed better.

Rude. Rude. Rude. Rude.

"The name of the guest?"

"Hughes."

I glanced at the keystrokes she made on the computer. Control F. Typical find command. She typed in the last name in the search function.

"Mr. and Mrs. George Hughes checked out earlier today."

"Right. Sorry. I meant their son, Hank."

Taylor seemed annoyed that she'd actually have to work, and with the likes of me, but she nonetheless entered another search into the computer.

"He also checked out."

I leaned my head, hoping to glance at her computer. "Are you sure?"

"Yes, I have a H. Hughes that checked out early this evening."

That could be Hank or Hunter. We still didn't know why Hunter had a room key to the Newport Heights. Not that there was a "we" anymore. My stomach twisted into a knot.

"Do you have another Hughes staying with you?" I casually leaned into the marble counter to catch a glimpse of the operating system.

She rolled her eyes and tilted the screen away from me. "Another Hughes? I already looked, and this one has checked out."

I spoke extremely politely. *Taylor may not care about five-diamond service standards, but I do.* "And thank you for checking," I smiled brightly, "but there may be a third room. Would you mind rechecking?"

She kept the screen tilted while her stiletto-tip nails on the keyboard sounded like they were scraping a chalkboard—and my last nerve.

"Oh." Her green eyes widened. She tucked her platinum-blonde hair behind her ear and glanced up with a half smile as way of apology. "We have a room for a Hunter Hughes, who's been with us for a while." She grabbed a pen, tore a sheet off her rainbow-colored memo cube, and after jotting something down handed me the note.

I glanced at the ten-digit number. "Oh, is this his cell?"

"No, it's the on-call front desk manager's number. The manager will meet you. Nonregistered guests have to be accompanied to the hotel room."

"Really? You don't call the guest's room to make sure the visitor is welcome?" Which in my case would suck because Hunter couldn't possibly answer any phone.

"No, we don't screen our guests' visitors. This is *the* Newport Heights."

"Of course," I said, and tempered my manner. *Pretty crap customer service if you need to be escorted to a room.* But still, it got me thinking. "What floor should I meet the manager on?"

She let out a long, exasperated sigh, glanced at the computer screen, and in a tone as annoying as her attitude said, "The third. His room is on the third floor."

Bingo!

I left before Taylor figured out what she'd revealed.

I'd bet my paycheck that hotel protocol required Taylor to call the manager, who would then meet me in the lobby. But Taylor's snobbery worked to my advantage. Now I knew which floor Hunter's room was on and I was armed with the manager's cell phone. Not sure what I'd do with it, but I had it. *Win.*

The Newport Heights wasn't a large banquet and convention resort hotel like the Waterfront. However, like the Waterfront, it was classified in the industry as a luxury, upscale hotel.

The Newport Heights was what many referred to as a boutique property—it was small, stylish, and located in the heart of luxury. Newport Beach, California, was home to John Wayne and only minutes away from his namesake airport and the Richard M. Nixon Presidential Library. Newport Beach was conservative and proud. The city was often said to be just to the right of Genghis Kahn.

I headed toward the elevators. I knew where they were because it was where Hank disappeared into after I introduced him to church. Or rather, the beach. It didn't much matter anymore, because the man wanted nothing to do with me. *How did it go bad so fast?*

The obvious answer was the MUM stick and the e-mail. I knew it. Hank knew it. The only person who didn't know it was Mr. Harpington, and after he suspended me without pay, I was glad I didn't reveal my source. I'd rather have driven myself to the poorhouse than drive another nail into Hunter's coffin.

The gold-coated elevator door opened, and I hopped inside.

I quickly pressed three and disappeared from view before Taylor or the on-call front desk manager was the wiser. The elevator quietly opened to the third floor, whose vibe was like the rest of the property—distinctly fashionable. The interior design matched the chic elegance of the exterior architecture. While each room had an ocean view and was equipped with a computer like at the Waterfront, the Newport Heights conveyed a different feel. It was sleeker, more contemporary, and downright progressive. It was like comparing a Rolex to a Timex. When it came to style and technology, Newport Heights had the Rolex on luxury and computers, and the Waterfront had the cheap knockoff version. And like a Rolex, the downside to exclusivity was cost. The Newport Heights wasn't cheap.

I had no clue which room Hunter had on the third floor, but I knew the guestrooms were individually decorated with unique personalities. I only hoped that there was a room on the third floor with the personality of an overachieving dreamer.

I slowly walked down the hallway that had a strong Newport influence. Artwork of Laguna and Newport Beaches hung on the walls, and a framed portrait of a bowl full of oranges oddly reflected the fullness and vibrancy of Orange County. The décor was as particular as the amenities, which I knew were top shelf. The Newport Heights and the Waterfront Point were competitors down to the thread count in the sheets. We always wanted a higher thread count, a higher occupancy rate, and higher customer satisfaction rating, because each one led to the other.

"If I was Hunter, which room would be mine?" I crept past each door, hoping for a sound or clue.

I had to find a room that was an extension of Hunter, which made me think of Hank. And while they acted nothing alike, one more flirtatious than the other, Hunter and Hank had one thing in common—they were tall. Hank was taller than Hunter, but if they were a guest they'd want something big with plenty of room.

"A suite!"

It was a total longshot because while a suite may reflect Hunter's personality, it didn't take into account that I was in a hotel. Perhaps the room that best fit Hunter was already taken by another guest. Or perhaps when Hunter booked the room, he was thinking only that he needed a space, and told them to just assign him anything. Still, despite the odds, I knew Hunter's room was somewhere on the third floor. And somehow a suite felt like one of those hunches Katie always talked about. I hoped I was right.

I aimed toward the end of the hallway where the suites were usually located. A cleaning cart was tucked in the corner of the T-shaped foyer, but no cleaning person was in sight. I quickly rummaged through the cart, hoping to find a passkey, but came up empty.

"No surprise there," I mumbled. Security at any hotel was first and foremost. A housekeeper that left a passkey on their cart was as good as fired.

I leaned my ear against the door of suite 313. There was no sound. I rapped my knuckles against the door. No one answered. I dropped my bag to the floor, slid down the door, and sat with my back against it.

"Okay, Hunter, I need your help." Tears stung my eyes and I quickly blinked them away. "So… I've really made a mess of things with your brother, and I don't even know what I'm doing here. Hank told me to leave him alone, now he's gone, and I'm here. And I really don't know what to do. I keep thinking that if I could find your room, I could somehow make things right with Hank." I shrugged. "I know that's crazy. But my gut tells me you didn't have a room here for nothing. So, if you have any ideas, I'm open." I exhaled, and on the inhale the sweet, perfumed air that hotels piped into the hallways crept into my nose. "And now the smell of grapefruit is making me hungry. Hunter, this is not going anywhere as planned. But I'm sure I don't have to tell you that."

I crossed my legs, closed my eyes, and took a moment. *Maybe this is where everything ends. Maybe it's time for me to let go.*

CHAPTER **TWENTY-SEVEN**

"Hey, Hank, how are ya?" Ollie's voice felt like a hug.

I shrugged and held my iPhone to my ear. A hurrying traveler brushed past me with his suitcase and laptop bag. "I was wondering if you could pick me up at the airport."

"Absolutely. You coming home?"

Home? I always associated "home" with Hunter. We grew up together and never grew apart. With him gone, I not only felt lost, I also felt homeless.

I watched the man who wasn't much older than Hunter and packed equally as poorly. His suitcase had the tail of a shirt sticking out the side and his laptop case wasn't buckled. Combined with his untied high-tops, he was an accident, and a lawsuit, just waiting to happen.

"Well, I'm at the airport," I said.

"Buddy, what's going on?"

It's why I called Ollie. He was our high school and college quarterback. It was second nature for me to follow his lead. And now I needed that direction.

I walked toward a row of uncomfortable looking seats and sat down. "I really don't know."

"When my mom died...." Ollie paused. "Man, it was rough. She was taken so suddenly."

My chest radiated with an intense heat that made it hard to breathe. "Do you remember when that dick from Oregon State stomped on my back after I sacked their quarterback in the playoffs?"

"Oh, you mean when he tried to pull a football version of a Christian Laettner on the field and step on your back. Yeah, I remember. And thankfully unlike Laettner, that douche was ejected. Then he whined to the newspapers and called what he did to you payback for your supposed illegal sack earlier in the game?"

"Yah, that one." I laughed. "The guy stomped so hard on my back, I felt it through my chest. Well, my chest feels like that."

"Buddy, that's to be expected. You just had a big blow. It was a huge hit to lose Hunter like that."

I paused. "I can't get on the plane." I lowered my head and tears fell on the red and blue carpet.

"Okay. Okay."

My football captain was always there to rally me after a loss, but this was different.

"I met this girl and...."

"Carmen, right? The one you ditched after the beach."

I chuckled.

"Didn't she try to help Hunter?"

"Yah."

"So, what's going on?"

I glanced at the clock above the departures and arrivals board. My flight boarded in twenty minutes. "I've got my bag beside me, my ticket's in my back pocket, and I'm even in the front section to board."

"But…?"

"My head wants to go, but my heart doesn't, and my feet won't move." I shook my head and pinched my eyes. "I really like this girl. Shit, I don't know how it happened, but it did."

"Does she know?"

"Fuck no."

Ollie laughed. "Well, I can see why you're having a hard time getting on the plane."

"It's not that."

"Okay."

"I basically told her to leave me alone."

"Oh, so you pulled a fumblerooski. Sure, that always works with women. What were you hoping? That another player on your team would pick it up and run the other way?"

The fumblerooski was a trick play in football where the quarterback intentionally left the football on the ground, and those of us on the line attempted to distract and confuse the defense by pretending another player was actually running the ball. It was a deceptive play and often worked in gaining significant yardage.

"I'm not that stealthy and you know it." I laughed. "And I wasn't trying to have someone else complete my play.

I'd never do that. I left the ball—or Carmen—on the field because she made me mad. And I got angry. I found out she sent the files Hunter was working on to herself."

"It takes a lot to anger you."

"Damn straight it does. But when someone I love is taken advantage of, then…." My jaw clenched and my fists tightened. "It pisses me off."

"How'd this Carmen gal take advantage of Hunter? I get that she e-mailed herself his files. Did she know what Hunter was working on? I mean, like was she stealing his software programs?"

"No, she didn't know what was on the files. Hell, she didn't even recognize a profit and loss statement. Not that's she stupid. Because she's not. She's really smart. She actually figured out a way to access Hunter's files. And you know how hard Hunter protected his shit. We were in the computer lab at her college when she figured out a way to download them."

"That's great."

"I know. So, if she wanted his files she could've asked for them. I mean, sure, she was already way late for work and we had, well, uh, we hooked up, but—"

"Did you? In a college computer lab. That's a first."

I shook my head and laughed. "Yah, it was pretty great. But then afterward she e-mailed herself the files. What the hell is that? You know me. I'd give anyone the shirt off my back."

"Does she know that?"

I shrugged. "Come on, Ollie. It's me. How would she not

know that? Especially after we were together."

"Buddy, I hate to be the one to shatter the image you have of yourself or of women, but first, you're kind of big and intimidating. And second, maybe Carmen freaked out. Maybe the two of you hooked up and she freaked. It happens. *Trust me*, it happens."

I slowly nodded. I knew Ollie and Kelsey had had their ups and downs before they found their happily ever after. "Yah, okay, so?"

"Is it at all possible that Carmen freaked out and in panic she exercised poor judgment? So instead of asking, she just sent the files to herself? You told me she's a computer geek like Hunter. That seems like something Hunter would do. Act first. Think later. And before you say anything, I'm not saying that you wouldn't have been approachable, and she *should* have asked you, but it doesn't sound like she was thinking too clearly." Ollie's hearty laughter caught me off guard. "Hell, Hank, it's not every day a girl gets a little bit of Hank the Tank."

"That's true," I said, smiling. "I am pretty selective about who I'm with."

"Sure, if you want to call it selective, I'll give you that."

I grinned. Nothing like getting sacked by the quarterback. "You're probably right. She probably wasn't thinking too clearly. I mean, like you said, after a little Hank the Tank, who would think clearly?" I burst out laughing, and the release felt good.

"There you go. That's what I like to hear. You probably spun the girl for a loop and she wasn't thinking straight.

Again, not cool, but not a deal breaker."

And there it was. The truth. No bullshit. Just the straight-up facts.

"Yah, what Carmen did pissed me off, and I know that Coach Gullberg would say beneath that anger, I was hurt. Stupid Coach and his classes in psych. I think Reid's the only one who got anything out of his lectures on human development. But—" I exhaled. "—you're right. It's not a deal breaker. I was hurt. Fuck, I hate saying that."

"Who does? Hurt sucks. But if Hunter taught us anything, it's that life's too short to waste being hurt— especially when you can do something about it. I wish we could change what happened to Hunter, but we can't. And that sucks. But Carmen? You can change the outcome of that. Buddy, life's too damn unpredictable."

"Yah." My voice lowered. "It sure as hell is."

"So, if you like this girl, fight *for* her, not with her."

I thought of my abrupt departure from the Security office. Carmen's blue eyes had all but lost their vibrancy. Her face had been ashen and her eyes had searched mine for a second chance, and instead of extending one, I'd left. I didn't fight for her, I fought with her.

"So, what are you going to do?" Ollie asked.

I rubbed my chin that badly needed a shave. "Offer my seat to one of the people on standby. You'd be surprised how many people want to go to Oregon."

"Hank?"

"Yah, yah, give up my seat and find her."

"And when you find her?"

I grinned. Ollie was nothing if not thorough. "When I find her, I'm going to…." I brushed my hand across the stubble on my head and glanced at the ceiling. Flags from different countries swung in the air-conditioning. "Fuck, Ollie, I don't know. I've never done this."

Ollie's hearty chuckle warmed me. "When you find her, tell her how you feel. Direct. Honest. Straightforward."

"And then what?"

I could practically hear my buddy smile. "When you tell the woman you like that you're *falling for them,* Cupid seems to work out the rest of the play. Just show up and give her your 100 percent. Nothing less, Hank. Give her your all."

Ollie's football huddles had always concluded with reminding us to give our all. If we each gave 100 percent, we were unstoppable. And we were. We led our high school to state, and our college team to the finals. His groundedness on and off the field was a foundation I trusted.

I exhaled. "Okay. I'm heading in."

"You got this."

"Hey, Ollie." I swallowed hard. "Hunter used to be my first call." Now it was Oliver. "Thanks for picking up."

"Hank, anytime. Like I told you, I'm just a call away. And when you do come home to Oregon, I'll bring Kelsey's new minivan."

"Minivan?" I walked toward the ticket counter, where I stood in line.

"Yeah, a minivan. And it's perfect for you, Carmen, and all her bags when she moves here."

For the first time, I knew where home was. It didn't matter if I was in Oregon or California, if the possibility for a future anything with Carmen existed, I'd move heaven and earth to make it a reality. Who knows, maybe our future something included a minivan.

I laughed. "A minivan, huh? I can't wait to see you driving that panty dropper."

"You know it. And shut the fuck up. It *is* a panty dropper. Anytime we get in the minivan, Charlie likes to undress down to his little boxer briefs so he can feel how soft the plush seats are on his legs."

"Oh, Ollie, that's beautiful, man." I was involved in the setup when Ollie proposed to Kelsey, and her son Charlie was a top-class kid.

"Buddy, when you find the woman of your dreams, every day is a thing of beauty. Don't get me wrong. I miss my mom every day, but with Kelsey and Charlie in my life, it hurts a little less."

I nodded. "When I'm with Carmen, the loss seems like it's manageable. And—" I paused. "—I don't seem so lost." I cleared my throat. "Hey, I'm next in line. I'll call you later. Thanks, Ollie."

"Anytime."

CHAPTER **TWENTY-EIGHT**

"Ms. Hughes?"

I opened my eyes and wiped the drool from my mouth. *Shit, I fell asleep.*

"Are you Ms. Hughes? I got a text from our front desk that you were locked out." His gold name tag read Bruce, and his olive-colored suit read management.

God bless Taylor's stupidity.

"Uh, yes, thank you, Bruce. I seem to have misplaced my key card, and…." I rolled my eyes for good measure. He extended his hand to help me stand. "Thank you."

I picked up my backpack and slung it over my shoulder.

"Well, let's get you inside. I'm so sorry you had to wait. We were looking for the driver of a truck who just left their car on the front drive."

"Really? Who would do that?" *Oh, dear God, what did they do with my truck?*

The man shook his head. "It happens more often than you think."

"Huh." I tucked my tank top into my jeans and tried to look more presentable. But hell, this was Orange County. For all he knew my white tank and faded jeans were shabby chic and cost more than a week's stay at the resort.

"Yeah, a lot of surfers leave their cars because they know we won't tow them in the event they're guests."

"Oh." I smiled and stepped aside while he approached the door to the suite. "So, what happens to those cars? The ones without drivers?"

"We valet them, and when the surfers return they usually don't mind paying for the parking, because it's still cheaper than a parking ticket or tow. And it's much more affordable than a monthly parking pass at the city or state beach."

I nodded. *Smart surfers.* I thought of Hank, and the ache in my chest returned. *Oh, Hank.* If we had just left the college and paddled out to the surf together. *I would have followed you anywhere.* Instead, I screwed things up so badly.

The door to the suite opened. "Housekeeping has maintained the room, although they said it's been a while since they've had to change the towels or bedding."

I nodded. "We're a green family." I smiled, thinking of Hank's jersey and his beloved Oregon. "We prefer to conserve water and reuse our towels."

"Of course. That's very conscientious. I wish more of our guests did that."

"Thank you."

"I'm sorry you had to wait. May I send up a bottle of wine and perhaps a fruit and cheese platter?"

I thought of Katie and how she'd respond. "That would be lovely."

"Wonderful. I'll contact Room Service. Is there anything else you'll need?"

I glanced toward the main room in the suite. A laptop was positioned beside a telephone. "I believe my husband took the password with him. Would you happen to have the Wi-Fi access and password for the computer?"

"Oh, that's not our system," he said. "Your husband asked that our computer be removed for his own."

I placed my hands on my hips. "He's always doing something like that. Of course. I'm sorry, I've had a bit too much sun today. I didn't recognize his computer."

Bruce reached into his jacket pocket. "Here's the Wi-Fi password. We update it daily, but this will work until tomorrow morning."

"Excellent, thank you." I turned toward the door. "Oh, could I get a new room key? I'm afraid I left mine either in the sand or South Coast Plaza."

"Absolutely. Not a problem. I'll have one sent up with room service."

"Thank you." I stood inside the foyer of the suite and Bruce took his cue to leave.

When the door closed behind him, I tossed my backpack into the main room and waited a moment before sneaking a look in the peep hole. Bruce was halfway down the hallway, my truck was in valet parking, wine was on its way, and Hunter's computer was ready for me to solve the mystery of what brought him here.

The laptop opened to a home page with a screensaver of what had to be the Oregon Coast. There wasn't anyone in the beach shore print and the sky was marbled shades of lavender, like a field of wildflowers in the sky. *Who'd want to leave that?*

On the startup window a box surfaced for me to enter my password.

"Oh, course." I bit my lip. "Okay, let's try 'password.'" I typed "password," hit Enter, and a message instantly surfaced that I had not guessed the correct password. *Shocking.*

I pulled my iPhone from my back pocket, thumbed it awake, and scrolled my notes section for my class notes. The last semester of notes streamed past me until I found the one labeled "Brute Force." I clicked it open.

Brute Force

The method of applying a program to decode encrypted data such as passwords. Brute force requires the programmer to write a program that will attempt to log in via a brute force attack. Some programmers use an online password dictionary that contains millions of words and tries every word in it to break the password, but this is very time-intensive. Each word has to be entered one by one. Plus there's no guarantee it'll work.

"Okay, so I've got to write a snippet of code to do a brute force attack on the password." I drummed my fingers on the desk, trying to convince myself that it was that simple. Just a snippet. "So, it's got to be a program that will guess the password over and over." I stared at the ocean that broke along the shore again and again. I needed to build one helluva program wave to crash the computer's password. I glanced back at the laptop and the empty coffee mug beside the phone. "Well, one thing's certain. I'm going to need a lot of wine."

I was reaching for the telephone when the doorbell to the suite chimed. "Nice."

I opened the door to Hector, who looked like my cousin Julia's ex-husband, Juan Carlos. I knew he wasn't, but he had the slicked-back hair, big brown eyes, and dimple that made it easy for Julia to fall for him.

"Ms. Hughes?"

My chest felt heavy. *Oh, if only*. "Please come in."

Hector rolled the white linen-covered room service cart into the suite that was probably as large as my papá's condo. "Would you like me to uncork the bottle?"

I smiled. "Yes, please."

"Excellent."

Hector and I probably attended the same class on how to answer a hotel guest. Excellent. Perfect. Wonderful. Anything that confirmed the guest, even when they were difficult, was the soup du jour. It left a bad taste in my mouth, but the tips I pocketed from working half my shift was hard to argue. I fished a twenty out of my pocket and handed it to him.

"Gracias."

"De nada." The cycle of tips never ceased to amaze me. My earned tips went from one guest service provider, whether it was Hector, or Maria who gave the best pedicures in Costa Mesa, to another; the circle rarely broke. And I knew during my next shift, I'd earn back my twenty twofold.

While he allowed the bottle of merlot to breathe, he reached into his shirt pocket and handed me a room key.

"Ah, muy importante."

He nodded with a grin. "Yes, you can't get back into your suite without it." He proceeded to lift the silver dome from the plate to reveal an assortment of artisan cheeses, dried and fresh fruit, vegetable crudités, hand-cut chips, ranch dressing, and a crispy baguette elegantly arranged on a cheese board.

My stomach growled, and I placed my hand over it. "Perdóname."

Hector laughed. "De nada." He poured the wine into crystal stemware and handed it to me. Hector clearly knew that testing the bouquet was lost on me. It was a red wine with a cork, which would taste infinitely better than Papá's wine from a box. And it did. The smooth, rich flavor slid down my throat and would give me the liquid courage I'd need to write a program to perform my first brute attack on a computer password. But hell, today was a first for many things.

Sex with Hank. Suspended from work. Sneaking into his brother's hotel room. *Sure, why not?*

Hector left, and I returned to Hunter's laptop. I popped a grape in my mouth and began writing a program that would guess the password repeatedly until it cracked it. Writing the code wouldn't take as long as the program's brute force on Hunter's laptop. When and if written correctly, the program wouldn't quit until it revealed the password to let me access the computer. *All this, just to access the computer.* My interaction with Hunter had been brief, but from what I learned from how he programmed his MUM stick, he'd most likely inserted some malicious code of his own to ensure that whatever he had on this laptop wasn't revealed.

"Hunter, I'm not here by happenstance, but if I'm going to break into your computer, I'm going to need *your* help to make it happen."

I no longer questioned my sanity. If talking to a dead genius programmer helped me figure my way through writing a program for the first time, I'd gab on.

"Okay, so this program has to repeatedly guess the password over and over, until it breaks it." I grabbed another grape. "So, to do that...." Suddenly the thought of Mr. Harpington when he slammed his fist on the table surfaced. He was an ass and a persistent one. He kept trying to get information from me in different ways—first he was nice, then he was condescending, then he just threatened.

"All right. So, my attack has to be a continual hit on letters, numbers, and symbols, with multiple approaches until one works."

I typed a line of code, then leaned back on the legs of the chair and glanced at the screen from a distance. "What am I forgetting?" *I want the letters, characters, and symbols to be evaluated by the brute force attack. Letters. Characters. Symbols. Letters. Characters. Symbols.*

I slammed the chair down on all four legs. "That's it! I haven't identified the letters, characters, and symbols!"

In front of the code, I typed code to specify both lower and upper case letters, numbers, and symbols. Then I wrote the algorithm, basically instructing the computer to run every variation of letters, characters, and symbols until one unlocked his computer. I exhaled, took a long, slow sip of wine, and hit Enter. A stream of code scrolled down the computer screen at lightning speed.

"Oh, dear God, it's working."

My eyes blurred as every possible password combination ran down the computer like someone was spinning the screen. Code upon code upon code. Password upon password. The patterns came fast and furious. I couldn't settle my eyes on one before the screen filled with new possibilities.

I sat in front of the computer, mesmerized. All I needed to do now was ditch my tank top for a black hooded sweatshirt, my wine for a Mountain Dew Code Red, and the cheese and fruit tray for Cheetos and chocolate Zingers, and it would be official—a hacker was born.

CHAPTER **TWENTY-NINE**

Carmen wasn't at the Waterfront, and the front desk clerk wouldn't reveal her schedule. I knew her house, but I wasn't sure I could find her neighborhood. My parents' rental car was at the Waterfront waiting for the rental company to arrive and return it for a hefty surcharge, but when I made my grand exit after meeting with Carmen and Harpington, I could only do it in one car. And I'd chosen Hunter's silver Mercedes. It was parked on the front drive of the Waterfront with my bag and the printout of Hunter's files in the back seat. I was walking toward it when someone looped their arm around mine.

"Hello, Hank. Looking for Carmen?"

Georgina.

I grinned. "As a matter of fact, I am." I glanced at her short, tight black skirt, gray T-shirt, black jacket, and what my buddy Jacob would call "fuck-me pumps," and with her arm looped in mine, I lightly elbowed her side. "So, where *you* headed?"

She nodded toward the Mercedes. "To my date. Drive me there, and I'll tell you where I think Carmen may be."

I raised an eyebrow. "Shouldn't your date be picking you up?"

Her reddish hair swung when she shook her head. "Oh, Hank. Being picked up has never been a problem. However, finding my way home, now, that's a different story."

I laughed. "You're serious."

"Si."

"So where am I taking you?" I opened her door and waited for her to tuck her long legs inside. "Are you and Carmen related?"

She laughed. "No, but we grew up together."

The car idled while Georgina flipped down the visor, dug through her purse, and withdrew a compact and brush.

"So where are we going?" I slowly rolled down the horseshoe-shaped front drive and headed toward Pacific Coast Highway, because everything in Huntington Beach seemed to intersect with PCH. Or Beach Boulevard. But my guess was that Georgina had a date waiting for her at some club off PCH. The magazine in my hotel listed about a dozen hot spots for tourists.

"Turn right and head north toward Seal Beach."

"Cool. Haven't gone that way up the coast." The lights on Huntington's pier shone like candles against the evening sky. Surfers paddled away from the beach into the dark waves that looked like sheets of glass beneath the early light of the moon. Glimpses of the tips of their boards were visible when they rode to shore.

"What a great town." I slowed behind the procession of cars lining up outside a faded red brick two-story brownstone.

"Surf City, baby." Georgina carefully held a black-pointed pencil to her eye.

I nodded toward the brick building that vibrated with sound. "What's that?"

Georgina didn't even look away from the mirror. "The Golden Cub. It's pretty chill."

"Club?"

"Brewery, live band, oldest music hall in Huntington. A lot of bands got their start there."

Cars turned onto Main Street and the parking structure for the Golden Cub. As we drove past, I glanced at the entrance. "It doesn't look pretentious." No velvet rope or bouncer.

"It's not. That's why the locals like it. If you want to hear good music and drink a fairly inexpensive IPA with the waves in your backyard, the Golden Cub's the place."

"Huh."

"Yeah, and before you even think of taking Carmen there, don't."

"Why?" I drove past Main Street and continued on PCH.

"Carm's not a nightclub kind of person. She's a homebody. If she's going to go out at night, it's to surf. Riding the surf at night is her jam—especially since no one can see her wipe out." Georgina laughed. "My *chica* doesn't like to do anything unless she can do it perfect."

"It's more dangerous at night."

Georgina stopped looking into the vanity mirror and arched a perfectly shaped eyebrow. "Have you met Carmen? Danger's her middle name."

I laughed. "Lame, but you're right. She's quite the little rule breaker, isn't she?"

"Hank, you have no idea what you're in for."

When I said nothing, Georgina pounced. "Ay Dios mio! You do!"

I remained silent.

"Hank, Hank, Hank." Georgina slowly shook head. "Didn't know you had it in you."

I smiled, but my lips remained shut.

"Well, that might explain why she was so upset when she left. I thought it was because she got suspended without pay, but—"

"What?" My foot hit the brake while my other foot pushed in the clutch so we wouldn't stall. Still, it was abrupt, and Georgina braced her arm against the dash.

"*Pinche cabrón*, are you trying to kill us?"

"Carmen was suspended? I thought Harpington was just blowing smoke to impress me. I didn't think he'd go through with it." Cars honked behind me but I didn't care. I stopped in the middle of PCH beside a sign for Bolsa Chica Wetlands on one side and an entrance to the beach on the other.

"I thought you knew."

"No." I shook my head. "I knew Harpington read her work e-mail and wanted to know where she got the files, but when I left I figured it was over."

Georgina gently placed her hand on my shoulder. "This isn't a safe place to just stop."

I put the car in first and picked up speed.

"When Carm wouldn't tell Mr. Harpington how she got your brother's files, he suspended her without pay. He said her actions threatened the security and integrity of the hotel and its guests."

I slammed my fist against the steering wheel. "That's bullshit."

"Agreed. She tried to save your brother's life, and it's as if Mr. Harpington conveniently forgets that."

"It's crap. How was she? You saw her before she left?"

"I did. She came to the IT office and told me how she accessed your brother's files by basically using a MUM stick hack, which was pretty badass. I wish I had thought of it. Would have saved us a lot of time."

"And maybe Carmen her job."

Georgina waved her makeup brush at me. "Uh-uh. Don't put what she did on me. That was all Carmen."

"*Why* did she do it? I would have given her the files if she asked for them." It was the question I couldn't seem to answer.

"Carmen's impulsive. She does things and thinks later."

"My buddy Ollie said the same thing about my brother. He thought maybe she was like Hunter. Act first. Think later."

Georgina unscrewed a black tube and held the wand to her eyes.

"Why do you wear so much makeup?" I seemed to

forget my filter around Georgina. "I'm sorry. That came out wrong. What I meant to say is that you're really beautiful. You don't *need* makeup. You're prettier than all that crap. Carmen doesn't wear any. Or if she does, I can barely tell."

She turned and her face softened. "You play football?"

"Yah. University of Oregon offensive linesman. Weak side tackle. My job was to protect the quarterback's weak side."

"And when you played in a game, did you ever go out without your helmet, jersey, shoulder pads, cleats, jockstrap, or uniform?"

I laughed. "No. Without my gridiron gear, I'd get hurt."

"Well, without makeup I could get hurt. Makeup is my protective gear from the haters."

"Who would hate you?" A Jack in the Box on the corner of PCH and some cross street streamed past us. Grilled meat and the heavy aroma of fried onions assaulted the air. *Damn, that smells good.* I glanced at Georgina. "Seriously, who would hate you?"

She stopped blushing her cheeks and highlighting her eyes. She sat with her hands in her lap, and the car became unnervingly still. "Hank, I'm gay. When I turn down a man and end up on the arm of a woman, it doesn't always go well. If I can give them one less thing to attack, I will."

My shoulders dropped. "I didn't know."

"Most people don't. They see a pretty woman and think she couldn't possibly be a lesbian."

I nervously laughed. "I guess I'm guilty of that."

"It happens all the time. I think the biggest misconception

about being a young gay woman is that people think once I 'come out' that I'll just be openly gay to the world. But it's not even remotely like that. I have to come out *all* the time. To every person I meet, I come out. Like with you. And there's no way to gauge a reaction. Sometimes it's ugly." Her voice cracked. "But I don't have to be."

"Georgie, you're a beautiful woman—inside and out."

"Thanks, Hank, but I'm still gay."

I laughed. "I wasn't hitting on you."

She leaned her head on my shoulder. "Ah, I know. I was just having fun. We both know your heart belongs to Carmen."

I gently placed my head on hers. "It does." I glanced at her. "So tonight? How'd you meet your date? And I still think she should pick you up."

Georgina pulled away and stuffed her makeup in her bag. "Her name's Trixie and we met online."

"Oh boy."

"No, she's a girl."

I laughed. "But online? Is that safe?"

"Hank, how old are you? Eighty? I've got this."

"I'm sure you do, but I've seen those lifetime television movies, and scary shit happens when people meet online."

Her laughter reminded me of Carmen. "It's nothing like those movies." She pointed toward a sign that announced Sunset Beach, and a row of restaurants tucked beside the harbor. "Pull in there. We're meeting for sushi."

"Cool."

"I know what you're thinking, two lesbians meeting

for fish. Ha Ha."

"That didn't even cross my mind. I was actually thinking I'm starving and sushi would *not even* come close to filling me up."

"I can see why Carmen likes you. You're not capable of lying."

"Not when it comes to food."

She laughed.

"So where do you think Carmen is?" I glanced at Georgina.

"Oh, that's simple. You left, but not before telling her quite emphatically that you wanted her to leave you and your brother's files alone. She was suspended for not revealing her source. She thought you left to fly home. And she knows that your brother had a key to the Newport Heights and one of the documents you downloaded was from the Newport Heights. Where would *you* go if you had nothing else to lose?"

"The Newport Heights to find my brother's room." I ran my hand across my head. "Why would she do that?"

"You don't understand Carmen if you have to ask that."

"She wants to help."

"Carmen felt awful. She made a stupid mistake. She e-mailed herself the files and she couldn't even tell you why. She just did. But the girl won't rest until she remedies this, and in her mind, it's unlocking why your brother had a room with our biggest competitor, and their profit and loss sheet."

"But why would she risk losing her job?"

"Men." Georgina slowly nodded. "You really are dense. Carmen's falling for you. And if you can't see that, then just go back to Oregon or wherever you're from. Don't waste my *chica's* time by being yet another guy who doesn't get her, and in that confusion tries to make her feel worse about who she is." Georgina pointed a red nail at me. "Carmen is all heart. She may not always use her head and think things through, but her heart is *always* in the right place."

"I'd never do that. I'd never make her feel worse about herself. I'd rather hurt myself than do that. I *really* care about her."

Georgina's eyes brimmed. "Dammit, Hank, I don't have time to redo my eyes." She whacked me on the shoulder. "No more of that."

I smiled. "Okay, but just so you know, my intentions are real. I adore Carmen. And even though how we met isn't even close to how I'd want to meet someone, I'm so happy she came into my life." The more I said it, the more my heart expanded until I thought it would burst.

"When two people connect, how and where isn't as important—only that they did." Georgina smiled and glanced toward the harbor. "Oh. There it is." Her normally calm, cool, collected demeanor shifted, and her energy spiked in a frenzy excitement. "Can you pull up to the front? I like to make an entrance. And this car will do just the trick."

I slowly pulled to the valet station, but before the lanky teen could open her door, I jumped out and did the honors.

A group of women walking toward the harbor-front

restaurant paused, but it wasn't me they noticed. Georgina's long legs appeared out of the car followed by her black skirt and black jacket that flapped back in the wind. That's when I noticed her gray T-shirt had something written in pink. I quickly glanced at what it said. "Breakfast in bed, please."

"Nice shirt," I whispered in her ear.

She threw her head back and laughed. And every woman there wanted to be with her. I smiled. "Be safe," I said in a low voice. "And if you get in a jam, call Carmen."

"Carmen?" She looked at me quizzically.

"Yah, wherever she is, I'll be right there beside her."

Georgina smiled. "Just as it should be."

CHAPTER **THIRTY**

A series of password combinations continued to flow nonstop on the screen. Two hours later, the program hadn't stopped spitting out amalgamations, nor identified Hunter's password. I knew the code I'd written worked, I just didn't know if it was strong enough to break his password.

The bottle of wine was half empty. The fruit and cheese tray was picked through. I pulled my hair into a twist and tied it behind my head in a messy bun.

"I've got to get out of here. If I stare any longer, my eyes will either dry up, bleed, or go blind. To save my sight and my sanity, I've got to leave this monastic cell of a hotel room."

I texted my cousin Julia that I wouldn't be home for the night, but I hadn't quite figured the rest of my plan. When Mr. Harpington suspended me from the hotel without pay, Security made me clean out my locker. I grabbed my backpack, threw it onto the bed, and hopped on the king-size splendor and dumped the contents of my bag onto the ivory satin duvet.

Tampons. Pads. Lip gloss. Deodorant. Baby powder. Flip-flops. Sweats. T-shirt. Jeans. Everything to get me through an incredibly dull weekend alone at home. Or the hotel. *This is definitely the opposite of what you'd pack for a romantic getaway. This is more like a platonic stay-away collection.*

"I thought I had…." I looked inside the backpack. "There it is!" In the bottom of the backpack, a white string glowed. I turned the bag inside out and unhooked the bikini entangled with the inside zipper. When it released, my favorite bikini, which I kept at the hotel for meal breaks on the beach, was in my hand. I jumped off the bed and headed toward the bathroom.

I pulled on my sweats, Ramones T-shirt, and grabbed the suite key off the desk. *Now to find a surfboard and wetsuit.*

"Good evening, sir, how may I help you?" She flipped her name tag so that Norma was no longer upside down.

"Well, Norma, my card key doesn't appear to be working anymore." I reached into my jeans and withdrew the hotel key that Carmen and I stumbled upon in Hunter's glovebox. We both knew it belonged to the Newport Heights, but not which room.

"Excellent. May I see some identification?"

"Of course." I pulled my Oregon-issued driver's license and handed it to the woman at the front desk, who had to be my mom's age. Props to the hotel for not discriminating against age.

"Hughes?" She squinted at the card.

"Yes, Hunter Hughes," I said, even though the ID was mine.

"Yes, yes, of course." She typed my brother's name into the computer and then placed the card into the key card system. "Oh, it looks like your wife recently had to get a new card as well."

"My wife?"

Norma glanced up from her computer. "Yes, apparently she locked herself out or misplaced her key?"

Carmen. I chuckled. "She's always up to something."

"It happens. Least we don't need to issue you a new card. Sometimes they charge for that." She wrinkled her nose as if the mere suggestion disagreed with her. "I'll just reprogram your card key. Sometimes the electronic strip from other credit cards in your wallet can deactivate them. You may want to put it somewhere else." She was so much like my mom it was spooky.

"Thanks, I'll do that."

She waited until the key card system flashed green. "Here you go, Hunter. That should get you into suite 313."

A suite, nice. "Thank you, Norma." I smiled. In the time I'd driven from Sunset to Newport, I'd upgraded to a suite and my Facebook status had changed from single to married. *All I need now is a minivan.*

###

"If you don't mind squeezing into a junior-sized wetsuit...."
He held the wetsuit. "I mean, it's only ankle busters at
this point. It's not like you're going to be doing much."
His concierge name tag read Tim, and he had all the
characteristics of a surfer: his hair was white blond, his
body had that beautiful, natural golden tan, and he dropped
"ankle busters" into the conversation. A die-hard surfer
wouldn't bother with tonight's small waves that crashed
at your ankles. Tim would hold out until morning for the
larger, optimal waves.

"Uh, Tim, that looks really small."

"Hold up." He jogged to the front desk and disappeared
behind the door that most likely led to the back of the hotel,
leaving me alone at the concierge desk.

I rolled my neck, but the kink just wouldn't release.

"May I?"

Hank? I spun.

His greenish-brown eyes shone along with his smile.

"You're here." My heart skipped a beat.

"I'm here."

"How did you know...?"

"Georgina helped piece it together, and then Norma at
the front desk told me my wife lost her room key."

I felt my face burn.

He cupped my shoulder and my body relaxed. "It's okay.
I'm not upset."

"I know, but you told me to leave things alone and...."

"You decided you just couldn't stay away."

I scrunched my face. "I once told your brother I was kind of a rule breaker. I guess I forgot to tell you."

"And I bet Hunter loved that—finding a fellow rule breaker."

I smiled. "I think he did."

Hank shook his head. "What am I going to do with you?"

"Surf?"

Tim returned with a wetsuit draped across his arm. "Oh, hey, should I look for one for you? You a shreddah?" He cocked his head toward Hank, who smiled.

"I do okay."

"Oh, surf with me."

He raised an eyebrow. "Do you *really* want company?"

"Are you serious?" I stared into his eyes to see if he was joking, which he wasn't.

He leaned toward me and lowered his voice. "Yah, I know how the beach is kind of sacred for you and all."

"That's why I took you there. And I want us to go back." I looked at him. "So, will you surf with me?"

"You betcha. I'd never miss a chance to surf with my wife."

CHAPTER **THIRTY-ONE**

Carmen tossed her flip-flops beside the stack of towels Tim provided us, and yanked off her sweats and band T-shirt to reveal a white bikini that could only be described in one word—breathtaking—which pretty much explained what happened to me. I knew I looked like a slack-jawed, open-mouthed goldfish that had jumped out of its bowl, but I couldn't seem to catch my breath or close my lips.

"What?" She glanced at her top. "Is my boob sticking out?"

I shook my head. "Uh, no."

"Oh. Then what's wrong?"

"Nothing. Absolutely nothing." The lights from the hotel pool and patio shone on the dark skin that flashed beneath the vibrant white. "You're hot."

She grinned widely. "This is my favorite bikini."

I pulled her toward me. "Mine too."

"So, you ready to catch some waves?"

"Something like that."

Carmen stood on her tiptoes and kissed me. "I missed you."

"I missed you too."

Her body tucked into mine. "I didn't mean to mess things up. I never should have sent myself Hunter's files." Her head rolled against my chest. "I'm so sorry I did that."

With Carmen in my arms, I wasn't sorry she felt that way; I was sorry I caused her to feel that way.

"Carmen, this is on me. Since Hunter and then I arrived at the hotel, you've been placed in unwinnable, untenable situations. From trying to save my brother's life to trying to decrypt his MUM stick, I would have bolted a long time ago. I'm shocked you're still here and want to help."

Her blue eyes questioned me uncertainly. Georgina was right. Carmen had been played one too many times by men that made her feel bad for their choices and in turn hers. *That ends now*.

"My buddy, Ollie and Georgie helped me see how much you and Hunter are alike. I *loved* my brother. Sure, he was impulsive,"—I smiled—"but his heart was always in the right place." I tipped her chin toward me. "I would have given you the files. But I understand why you didn't ask. I know my size can be intimidating, but I'm kind of a gentle giant. And when it comes to you, Carmen, I'd give you anything your heart desired."

"My heart only desires you."

I swallowed the lump in my throat, leaned down, and kissed her. Our lips met in a tender embrace.

A beautiful smile slid across her face. She reached

behind me and swatted my ass. "So, what color you got under there? Or are they the same ones I saw earlier today?"

"No, before I checked out of the hotel, I showered and changed. I thought I'd be traveling to Oregon."

"I'm *so* glad you aren't." And from the tender expression on her face, I knew it was true.

"Me too."

"So…." She tugged on my jeans.

"So… I'm going to freeze my ass off in nothing more than these Brazilian trunks and wetsuit."

"Nah. Once we start paddling out, you'll warm up."

I unsnapped my jeans and parted the fly. Carmen's eyes twinkled with anticipation, which made me laugh. "I hate to disappoint, but they're just black. Basic black."

"*Si*. But they're the Brazilian kind and that is *muy caliente*."

I turned around, placed my hands on my hips, and playfully shook my Brazilian butt at her. Carmen giggled.

"Ah, yah!"

I shook my head, reached for the smaller wetsuit, and tossed it to her.

"It'll be hard to miss us." I placed my foot into the leg of the wetsuit. A green neon strip ran down the side. Carmen's was lined with tangerine orange. "Well, I guess if surfing doesn't pan out, you could always be a highway flagger girl in this," I said while I zipped up her back.

"No way. It's awesome. Glow-in-the-dark wetsuits, too cool. I've only read about these. It allows us to see each other and I'll be able to watch you surf."

Her excitement was adorable and made my heart swell. I was falling—hard. I didn't know when I'd tell her, only that I would tonight. Ollie was right, life was too unpredictable.

We grabbed our borrowed surfboards and headed toward the glassy water, with waves that broke closer and closer to shore.

###

I paddled out beside Hank, whose board was twice the size of mine. Still, I kept pace with his arms that could double as oars. He kept looking back.

"Don't turn around to check on me or you'll lose power," I said.

"I'm not checking *on* you. I'm checking *out* your ass," he said with a smile.

I shook my head. "You're *loco*."

"I'd be crazy *not* to notice that sweet little apple bottom. Damn if I'm not hungry." He laughed, and my body flushed with warmth.

"Actually," he said. "I'm really looking for sharks. I figure if they spot you first they'll be so distracted by your butt cleavage I'll have time to swim back to shore."

I couldn't catch my breath for laughing so hard. "*Pendejo*. I'm in a wetsuit, they can't even see me. And I don't have butt cleavage." Though I still glanced behind me, which made Hank howl like a wolf in the moonlight.

"*Pinche cabrón*."

"Such language."

"Hey, you're the one that's going to leave me if you spot a shark."

The grin on his face made me want to slip off my board and onto his and smother him with kisses. "Yeah, sorry Carm. I can handle a lot of things, but I draw the line at sharks. Not a fan."

I giggled. "Good to know."

A wave rose in the distance. "Oh, if you see a wave, you want to be quick to catch it before it breaks so you have time to get up on your board."

He scooped a handful, which was more like a Hank-ful with his massive mitts, and splashed water in my face. I shook my head and wiped my eyes.

"Listen, missy, I may not know squat about computers and programming, but when it comes to sports, I'm the Bill Gates with mad skills. I'm the expert with experience. The top of my class. The one to beat."

"So, you *are* more than just an eating machine?" I playfully jested.

He raised an eyebrow, but the moonlight revealed his reddened cheeks.

"That's good to know," I said with a wink, "because you certainly couldn't be any worse at sports than you are at computers. Your Oregon upbringing may have given you the same pasty complexion as a computer whiz, but the physical comparison pretty much ends there. Hank, you could probably bench press a car while most hackers struggle to just move a CPU."

"Two cars. I can bench press two cars."

I giggled and placed the back of my hand to my forehead. "*My hero.*"

"You know it, baby. Always."

When we were past the white water and on the outer edge of the wave, we sat on our surfboards just outside where the waves broke. The tips of our boards faced shore. The night was clear and lit by a full moon that cast its light on the water. Sitting beside Hank with a full moon overhead was unexpected, exhilarating, and another first. I couldn't imagine being anywhere else or with anyone but him.

His hands skimmed the surface rippling the dark water between us. Everything about him was larger than life, yet beside him I didn't feel diminished. If anything, I felt beautiful, smart, cherished, and desired. His beastly manliness captivated me and provided a sense of security. I knew that wherever I went, Hank would always look over his shoulder to ensure my safety and well-being. He was a gentle giant who claimed my heart with his soft soul and generous warmth.

Hank spotted the approaching wave before I did. He popped down on his board and paddled toward it, catching the wave before it broke. As the wave grew in height, Hank moved faster. His arms paddled quicker than the wave moved. He pointed his board toward shore, placed his hands on the board in a push-up position, pushed himself up in one quick, fluid motion, planted his feet firmly on his board, crouched low to maintain balance, and when the wave crested a stream of neon green from his wetsuit accentuated his broad shoulders, beefy build, and powerful legs.

Watching Hank surf was a thing of beauty. Wherever this journey took us, there had to be a beach where we could be happy and together, and not merely content and miles apart on separate shorelines. Wherever Hank was, I wanted to be beside him.

CHAPTER **THIRTY-TWO**

The simplicity of a plain, white string bikini never looked so good. A classic, down to the triangle shapes that barely covered Carmen's full breasts. I wrapped a towel around Carmen and stared at a fire that glowed in the distance.

"I wish I had thought of that."

"Me too." Carmen tucked her chin, pulled the towel around herself, and tried to stop her teeth from chattering.

"We can go back to the room."

She shook her head. "No, I want to be with you on the beach."

"Carmen, you're freezing."

She turned into me. "Then change that."

I rubbed her shoulders through the towel and considered my options. I could run to the hotel and hope to hell they had a bonfire kit. If Norma and Tim were still on duty, I'd be in luck. But if they weren't, I risked colliding with someone at the front desk who knew I wasn't Hunter. Or…. "Don't go anywhere." I began to dart off, and then I stopped and held up my hand. "I'm *not* ditching you."

Her laughter followed me down the beach. My feet dug into the wet sand, making it hard to run. I did what I always did when presented with a physical challenge—I pushed past the discomfort. *No pain, no gain.* I raised my knees and took longer strides, until the fire came into view. A group that reminded me of Ollie, Kelsey, and our Oregon crew were camped around the fire.

"Hey, guys!" I announced myself before I approached. Ollie's reminder that my size was intimidating helped. At six-six and in a black wetsuit, I didn't want to be mistaken for the creature from the black lagoon and chased down the coast with s'more sticks and fire torches.

"What's up?" one of the guys said.

"I just went surfing with…." I rubbed my chin. Carmen wasn't my wife. I thought she was my girlfriend? "Listen, I went surfing with this girl I really like and now she's freezing. Would you have any firewood and matches you could spare?"

Three women who were Carmen's age, early twentysomething, jumped into action. One guy tossed me his lighter. "Take it."

"Thanks, man. I appreciate it."

"Sure. Any guy that'd surf at night with a girl, I'm not going to stand in the way," he said.

I laughed. "The things you do to impress a woman, right?"

The women loaded my arms with wood and placed a bag of marshmallows, a sleeve of graham crackers, and a chocolate bar on top.

"If you really want to be date-worthy," a redhead said, "make her a s'more then feed it to her."

I suddenly felt really hot, and I'm sure my face revealed my embarrassment. "Thanks. I think I'll stick to what I know—building the fire and getting her a stick for the s'mores." I nervously laughed and raised my armload of supplies toward them. "Thanks for the assistance."

"Oh my gosh!" Carmen shrieked. "What did you do?"

I smiled. "Just picked up a few supplies." I pulled off my wetsuit and tossed it beside our surfboards that stood in the sand and created a windbreak. I dug a wide hole in the sand and arranged the firewood, a few pieces of dry driftwood, and whatever sticks I could find into a tepee in the center of the hole. Carmen gathered rocks and placed them to form a ring.

I grabbed the thinner sticks, cupped my hand around them, and lit the ends. I tucked the kindling into the middle of the firewood tepee and it ignited without collapsing. I'd made a lot of fires on the beach in Oregon, but this was probably the most important one.

"Damn! Nice job, Hank."

Pride filled my chest. "You think that's something, just wait till you see what I have cooked up for dessert."

"I haven't even eaten dinner yet." She laughed.

"Me either. We're doing things a bit different tonight."

She cuddled beside me in front of the fire. "And here I thought I was the one that bent the rules."

"Bent? Carmen, you not only bend the rules, you spindle and mutilate them, but I will give you this, girl, you never *really* break them. You just come *really* close."

I once read that laughter was the best aphrodisiac, and the way Carmen laughed I knew I was tickling more than just her funny bone. She looked at me like I was Atlas, Ares, and Adonis, tall, dark, and handsome, all rolled into one.

Her towel dropped from her shoulders and the moon caught the white triangles that really did a poor job of covering her. She reached behind her neck, untied the strings, and the triangles fell like dominos. And I was mesmerized.

I still couldn't believe a woman like Carmen wanted to be with a big duff like me. It wasn't that I lacked confidence, but I knew when I was tipping my skis. It was one thing to have a one-night or one-computer-room stand, or even a short-term summer fling, but I wanted the possibility of forever with Carmen.

The way she revealed herself to me in the moonlight, I realized I may be a little bit over my skis, but she didn't seem to mind.

If you like her, fight for her, not with her. Ollie's voice in my head. Not fighting with her extended to not fighting the feelings welling inside me.

"Carmen, you're beautiful." I brushed her hair behind her ear.

She knelt in just her bikini bottoms, which made focusing nearly impossible.

"And smart." I grabbed her hands. "Carmen, you are so smart. You knew what to do when you found my brother, and I don't know anyone who would have done that." I swallowed. "From the moment I heard you on the phone trying to save his life, I knew there was something special about you."

Her blue eyes were as glassy as the ocean that serenaded us with the constant, tranquil beat of water caressing the shore.

"I wanted to meet you. I wanted to meet the woman I admired before I knew her. And when I met you, you were an unexpected surprise. I knew you'd be amazing, but I didn't know that your soul would touch mine. How could it? I was broken, and I never thought I'd feel whole again. But then you brought me to your house for dinner, and to your sanctuary by the sea." My eyes never left hers. "I left you that night at the beach because I didn't know what to make of it all. This perfect woman at the most imperfect time."

I lowered my head and felt my eyes burn from the salt water and tears. She gently placed her hand against my cheek.

"Hank, I understand. You explained this all to me."

"But I didn't tell you everything."

Her face questioned me.

I visually and mentally soaked in her perfect beach body and beautiful face, in the event that after what I told her, she opted to bail. "You are more to me than the woman that tried to save my brother. You're so much more." I felt my heart pound like I just ran the four-hundred-yard dash in record time. "Carmen." I held her hands tightly. "I'm falling for you, and it's not some passing thing. It's the 'I want the possibility of forever with you' kind of falling."

She pulled her hands free and wrapped them around me. "Me gustas, Hank, me gustas."

"Man, I hate to kill this mood," I said in her ear, "but does that mean you like me too?"

"Si." Her body shook against me as she laughed. "*Me gustas*. I like you, too."

The surfboards that stood in the sand not only blocked the wind, but also prying eyes. Carmen wrapped her legs around my waist and began kissing my neck. She was so petite, yet she fit perfectly wrapped around me. Her breasts pressed against my chest, and as our kissing intensified I slid my hand into her bikini bottoms.

"You've got such a great, tight little ass." I cupped her cheeks and she pressed into my erection.

"You're not so bad either." Her tongue trailed my chest and flicked across my nipples, spiking my desire.

I reached behind me for two of the dry towels.

"What are you doing?"

"I thought I'd move us to the sand."

She shook her head. "Move now and I'll kill you."

She pressed into me, rubbing herself against me. "Oh, right, got it. Sorry."

She giggled. "Just a warm-up, but...." Her back arched and my mouth covered her breast.

"Yes, yes. Right there."

I hiked my thumb into my trunks and pulled them down. She slid her bikini over until it resembled a sexy G-string, and mounted me in the moonlight. The surfboards blocked us from the hotel, but anyone combing the beach would spot more than they bargained for. But when Carmen dug her nails into my back, no one else existed. This was our beach. Our time. Our night. I cupped her ass, slowly moving her up and down against my hard shaft, which throbbed for her. Her body responded with a gush of wetness that welcomed me. She pushed my head toward her breasts. I covered her dark areola with my mouth and gently sucked on her nipple.

"Bite me." Her directive was in my ear.

All right then.

I cranked things up a notch, lightly bit her nipple, thumbed the other, and gently fingered her ass. Carmen's cries could probably be heard in Mexico, but I didn't care. This beautiful woman was savoring my cock, and I savored her delight. The more turned on she became, the harder I got. I would hold out until Carmen not only orgasmed, but was out of orgasms. I would last all night. I would outlast the fire.

Or maybe not. As Carmen moved faster and faster, sliding up and down on my cock, her tight, wet folds enveloped me.

"I want your balls inside me. I want *all* of you inside me," she cooed, and if I could have made it happen I would have.

My finger went deeper in her ass, and she clamped down on me.

"Oh God, suck me."

My teeth returned to her nipple, and her nails practically pierced my skin. I moved my other hand to her clit and began to rub her. She lit up with a fevered pitch. Her breathing intensified, her heart beat hard against mine, and I felt a marked increase in wetness. Her breathiness gave way to moaning that quickly escalated to guttural screaming, which was music to my ears. When she orgasmed, a rush of heat coursed through me. Her orgasms were so intense, and sent shock waves through her body and mine. When she hit the finish line, it was unlike anything I'd experienced, heard, or seen. An orgasm like that was so elusive it was urban legend. *Hell yes!*

"I love your cock." She clamped down, and I plunged what she loved so far inside her I thought she'd get her wish and my balls would accompany the ride.

"Hank—don't stop."

I wouldn't last all night or even till the fire died down, but I could last long enough for Carmen to hit it one more time. But she didn't make it easy. The more she teased the head of my cock, the harder it was to hold on.

She grinded, rubbing her clit against me. Sweat dripped between us. I dug my hands into her round ass just as she exploded; her body shook and trembled against me. I couldn't last any longer. I pulled her into me hard and erupted inside her with a loud, throaty burst.

CHAPTER THIRTY-THREE

"What's your favorite ice cream flavor?" I held my stick with two marshmallows into the flame and cuddled close beside Hank.

"Well, not burnt marshmallow." He laughed while he strategically assembled a rectangle of chocolate onto a graham cracker square and placed it on a flat rock beside me.

"Burnt marshmallows are the only way to make a s'more."

"I disagree." His stick was propped in the sand over the fire, where his marshmallows roasted like my *papá's* favorite rotisserie chicken, slowly over the open flame.

"That takes too long." I placed my charcoaled marshmallows on the chocolate and slid them off the stick with another graham cracker, squishing them together to complete my gooey sandwich. "This is quick and tasty."

"If my buddies were here they'd jump all over that."

"Quick and tasty?" I raised an eyebrow and sank my

teeth into the sticky, melted chocolate goodness.

"Yes, quick and tasty." Hank repositioned his stick to evenly toast his marshmallows.

"So, when do I get to meet these buddies?"

His eyes widened. "Wow. Anytime. I was serious when I said that I wanted the possibility of forever with you."

"I want that too. I'd like to see where this could go, but I'm just not sure how we make this work when—"

"We live on the same coast, but there's a thousand miles of beach between us?"

"Exactly." Suddenly I didn't feel hungry anymore. I placed my s'more on the rock and leaned my head on Hank, who lifted his arm and tucked me into him.

"Carmen, I'm not leaving California without you."

Heat flushed my chest with an ache that felt like happily ever after wasn't to be ours. "My family is in California."

His lips pressed into the top of my head. "Then I'll live here. I mean, as long as they have peanut butter chocolate ice cream, because to answer your earlier question, that's my favorite. They have that in California, right? Or is it too rich for the golden coast?"

"Hank." I shook my head. "Your family is in Oregon, and they need you right now."

Ice cream preference—chocolate, strawberry, or even peanut butter chocolate was no different than how we showed our emotions. Everyone had a different way to express their emotions, just like everyone had a different ice cream preference. Hank's was to wrap himself around me like he'd never let go, and I didn't want him to.

CHAPTER **THIRTY-FOUR**

"So… what I can't understand is the spreadsheet. The profit and loss sheet."

I sat beside Carmen at the desk in the suite. She wore my University of Oregon T-shirt that was at least four times too big for her. She wore green well and looked absolutely adorable. I smiled.

"What? Do you understand the spreadsheets?"

"Your accent," I said.

"What'd I say?"

"Spreadsheet sounded like spread shit."

Her neck turned red, and I knew her face was next. "*Sheet*. Shit." She giggled. "What'd you find?"

"You first. You're the one that broke my brother's password."

She smiled. "My first brute force attack and it worked!" She pumped her fist in the air. "After thousands of password combinations, who knew that your brother's password was bang hank at 55 bang."

"What's with the bang? Are you trying to make a point?" I chuckled.

"No, it's nerd language for an exclamation point, a bang or screamer."

"Seriously? You line these things up for me."

"Yes, and aren't you the gentleman for not capitalizing on them." She grabbed the pen and pad of paper from the desk and wrote !Hank@55! "That was your brother's password. What's the 55 represent?"

"The number on my college football jersey."

"Nerdy, but cool."

"Nerdy? Well, if anyone would know nerdy, it's a person getting a college degree in that field." I wagged a finger. "So, I'll let go of bang, but not screamer. I'm holding on to screamer."

I adored making Carmen laugh. It was a rich, joyful sound that warmed me from the inside out.

"So, since you were able to open his laptop, does that mean you can access his files and I can toss his MUM stick?" I grabbed the device from my bag.

"First, if you're going to toss a four-hundred-dollar MUM stick, would you mind placing it in my trash can?" She pointed toward a backpack on the bed. "And second, yes, I can open anything on his laptop because he didn't have the files on his laptop encrypted. And what it looks like…." Her finger moved across the touch pad. Her thumb right clicked open the two files we hadn't printed. Two budget reports surfaced. "It looks like more financial stuff?" she asked rather than stated.

"It's clear what we need to sort through this mess."

"Wine?" She scrunched her face. "Because I already drank a lot of it."

"No wine. Wine's for sissies. We need whiskey—with an 'ey' for the good stuff—steak, and potatoes."

Carmen glanced at the laptop. "It's almost midnight."

"Well, thank goodness this hotel has twenty-four-hour room service." I picked up the phone and didn't bother to locate the in-room dining button, I went directly for the operator. "Hello! This is Mr. Hughes in suite 313."

"Good evening, sir, how my I help you?"

"I'd like dinner brought to my room as quick as feasibly possible."

He laughed. "Right away. Let me connect you to Room Service."

I was on with Room Service long enough to order our dinner, and phone the front desk again. "Mr. Hughes here. Yah, Room Service doesn't appear to have any whiskey bourbon. Nor do they have scotch whisky. What I'd like is whiskey with an 'ey,' so that means anything bottled in Kentucky."

"Uh…."

I understood the hesitation. He was an hourly overnight front desk clerk wishing he hadn't picked up the phone. "Perhaps you can have your overnight manager go to your purchasing department, where they have a locked liquor cage. The on-duty manager will have the key, and tell him it's for Mr. Hughes, who has occupied your best suite for more than a week."

"Of course, sir. Right away."

"Thanks, buddy. I appreciate it. Oh, would you please make sure to bring the whole bottle and two glasses?"

Carmen's blue eyes widened. "*Ay caray.* An entire bottle?"

"Carm, we're having porterhouse. I can practically hear the sizzle from the porterhouse now. It happens when it's broiled with clarified butter and placed in an eight-hundred-degree oven. It's really two meats for the price of one—there's the soft filet mignon on one side of the bone, and the meaty sirloin on the other." I smacked my lips. "You can't serve anything but a Kentucky bourbon with a porterhouse. It'd ruin the meal."

"How do you know so much about food?"

"Yah, I know a lot of people think purchasing is simply shopping online, but a good purchasing agent makes informed choices, and the best way to make the most informed choice is to test the product. I've had the absolute best and worst food and beverage. I've tried every soap imaginable, and my hair has been washed in environmentally safe shampoo, baby shampoo—I've even used dog's shampoo. All to no avail, but at least I don't have to worry about fleas and ticks. Suffice to say, if it's offered at the Carlyle, I've had it first."

"That's the most excited or enthused I've seen you about your job."

I shrugged. "I like working for old man Carlyle and his twin boys, Reid and Oliver. Ollie works at his mom's property now, but you said it, it's a job. Sure, it's actually a career, but it's not like what Hunter had. Hunter was pursuing his dream, man. He was lit up about it." I looked at his laptop and the familiar tug returned to my chest. "Hunter did what he loved."

Her voice softened. "What do you love?"

I smiled. "Football."

"So, could you coach? I don't know what it's like in Oregon, but in California you have to have a coaching certificate or something like that. Tomás wants to coach soccer, so after he graduates college, he'll work toward that."

"It's pretty much the same. I have my college degree, and I'd have to probably earn my teaching certificate or something like that."

"Do it." She reached for my hand. "I mean it. Do it. You'd be a great coach."

"What about you? When do you graduate?"

"Well, technically I could graduate at any time. I've finished all my course work, but I was waiting for the summer graduation to walk with my classmates. I'm enrolled in a capstone class where we basically work independently on projects for our portfolio."

"So, would hacking a MUM stick and writing a brute force attack look good on this portfolio?"

"It'd be amazing, but I'd have to show my results, and that would mean revealing the contents of your brother's work. And," she scrunched her face, "I'm not sure that's such a great idea."

"Agreed. I'm sorry, but that would bring more eyes into this than we want." I slowly nodded. "Let's look at those other files."

She awakened the laptop and the two spreadsheets surfaced. "This is the forecast sheet for the Waterfront." I minimized the screen to review the other file. "And this is a forecast of the Newport Heights. How do you think Hunter got the forecast for the Newport Heights anyway?"

"Hunter could break into Fort Knox with a computer. But I imagine he found them on the Waterfront server. So, the question becomes, how did Harpington get them?" I glanced around the room. "Do they have a printer here?"

"The hotel might, but your brother didn't have one."

"That's okay. I'll work with the printed copies of what we have and if it's only two spreadsheets to view on the computer, that's nothing. Having to juggle nine spreadsheets is eight too many." I laughed.

"What can I do?"

I opened the internal envelope and handed Carmen half the stack. "I have no idea what we're looking for either, so we'll divide and conquer."

After two porterhouse steaks, a quarter bottle of whiskey, and nine financial spreadsheets, it was clear that Michael Harpington was up to no good.

"Harpington needed to know where his more successful competitor was making and losing money so he would know what areas of the budget he would need to pad with what looks like laundered money to artificially match the profit levels that were actually achieved by Newport Heights," I said.

"Money laundering? What does that mean?"

"Money laundering would explain why the hotel is far more profitable than its low occupancy rate would suggest. If he were siphoning money, it would explain why the hotel was far less profitable than its high occupancy rate would suggest. But the Waterfront doesn't have a high occupancy rate."

"Yeah, it does," Carmen said. "We're always at 90 percent."

"The forecast may claim 90 percent, but the other day when you called Katie in the computer lab, didn't you say the occupancy rate dropped to like forty?"

"You're right!" She pulled her hair back and tied it in a knot behind her head. "It went from ninety in the midmorning to forty by late afternoon."

I grinned. "Harpington is doctoring the forecast months in advance by comparing the hotel's occupancy rate with Newport's. And I'm pretty sure he either paid someone at the Newport Heights for the files or he had one of his IT wonders hack their system—although I doubt any of them are that good."

"Georgie is, but she wouldn't hack for him."

"True. Georgie could probably get into the Newport Heights system, but like you said, she wouldn't. So, the most likely scenario is that he got someone in the accounting office who needed some extra money and felt no loyalty to the hotel to download their P&L statements and forecasts for him."

"Okay, so once Mr. Harpington had those, what did he do?"

"First, he forecasted high occupancy rates, and then as the date of the event approached he dropped the rooms so the occupancy rate reflected the actual numbers but it looked like a high cancellation rate, not a shortage of bookings."

"Why would he do that? Even you said the Waterfront wasn't cheap."

"Making a failing hotel profitable makes Harpington a corporate savior. Doing so via money laundering makes it easier than actually doing the hard work of turning around a once-profitable luxury hotel that used to be the 'jewel of the coast' but has fallen on hard times and is now a rhinestone resort."

"You keep saying money laundering. I know you're not talking about Pablo in housekeeping actually laundering the money." Carmen's high-pitched giggle was the effect of good bourbon.

I laughed. "No, he's not actually washing money. Okay." I grabbed the pad of paper with Hunter's password written and flipped a page. "Living so close to Las Vegas, you've probably heard of failing casinos. It's not just limited to Vegas. It could be Atlanta. Reno. Wherever there's casinos, like hotels, it's an industry."

She nodded.

I drew a series of boxes to resemble hotels along a long strip. "Okay, so there's hundreds of casinos. And many in the industry claimed that the *entire* casino industry was hit by the 'bad economy.'" I put a single slash through each of the hotel boxes.

"Okay."

"And some of the casinos really did fail." I marked the slash with an X, wiping out a few casinos. "The gaming industry is a prime target for moving large sums of money. And while some casinos legitimately failed, others were hit by the Justice Department with anti-money laundering violations." I circled a random group of hotel boxes to signify the latter.

"What's that?"

"There are federal rules and regulations that casinos, hotels, every business you can imagine, have to follow. Casinos are often targeted because they cater to wealthy folk, but when money comes from overseas, the risk of introducing illicit money into the US financial system can be a blind spot."

"Because the hotels and casinos want to cater to them?"

"Exactly. There isn't any business—or good business— that doesn't want to impress its customers, but it can't come at the risk of *laundering* money into our country."

"So that's what it means. But how does it happen?"

"With casinos, they gamble. They use the money made from illicit industries, like running drugs, and play the high-end tables. Other times, dummy corporations are established in the US. These fake corporations open the door to launder a lot of overseas money that's pushed through US banks through false receipts and fake businesses. Once the money goes through our banks, it's sent back to wherever it originated, which is how the 'laundering' part works. Basically, the money returns looking like legitimate money because it's been laundered or washed through profits from a fake company."

"Wow."

"Yah, done right money launderers are very successful and evade detection."

"How do you know so much about this?"

"As the Director of Purchasing, I have to ensure that the products and foods we purchase are from legitimate businesses. It'd be all too easy to buy our soap cheaper from company X, only to discover company X is using us to clean their money."

"I know you'll make a great football coach, but damn, when it comes to purchasing you really know your stuff."

I shrugged. "When I go in, I go all in."

She playfully smiled. "I've noticed."

There was never a dull moment with Carmen. I grinned.

"So, it's a real sleight-of-hand then," she said.

"It actually can be. White-collar crime is very sophisticated. Examining the finances is key." I typed "money laundering" into the Google search bar and myriad hits surfaced. "It happens in nearly every country. And usually when someone gets close to discovering the truth, their employment is terminated or suspended because they pose a security threat." I glanced at Carmen, whose mouth was agape. "Yah, sound familiar? Your suspension without pay isn't by coincidence. I'm sure Harpington thinks you knew what he was up to."

"He said my actions threatened the security and integrity of the hotel and its guests." She crossed her arms over her chest.

"Carmen." I began to laugh. "It wasn't you, it was him."

"Ha. Ha."

"Sorry." I refilled my whiskey glass. "Hunter discovered what Harpington was doing by comparing the Waterfront's forecast sheets to the profit and loss statements. They didn't line up and they should." I fanned the spreadsheets on the table between us. "I mean, there'll always be a degree of difference, but not this great." I pointed to a three-month forecast compared to a month-end report that varied significantly. "Harpington is padding the forecast with room rentals where he charges the deposit and a one-night room charge in advance, and then on the day the guests are slated to arrive, he releases their rooms. This allows him to keep their deposits and possibly a night's lodging because they didn't cancel within the designated window for cancellations. You do have a cancellation policy, right?"

"Do we ever. We have a 'one-night penalty' policy, which charges a cancelation fee equivalent to one night's stay at the hotel plus their deposit. And some guests are required to prepay with a nonrefundable hotel reservation because of past problems collecting their payment. Or so we've been told at our weekly forecast meeting of guests coming to the property. So the guests that are under our prepay have to pay for the entirety of the reservation at the time they book and it's totally nonrefundable."

"Yah, see it's a perfect setup," I said. "Most hotels have

a 'cancel by certain date' policy which gives travelers the option to cancel their hotel reservation free of charge up and until a certain date. But with the types of reservation policies you described, Harpington has total access to use the deposit account and one-night room rental account for his money laundering." I rubbed the stubble on my chin. "Whoever he's laundering money for, he's likely getting some kind of kickback for it."

"Or maybe he's just trying to save the hotel. His ego is attached to each of the properties in his chain," she said.

"You're probably right. I don't deny that his ego is wrapped in this, big time."

"So, what I don't get is why Hunter had this suite at the Newport Heights?" she asked.

"He was smart." Pride filled every inch of me. "You don't want to do the analysis of corporate espionage at the place you're surveilling. And after Harpington told me they created a special IP address for Hunter, that meant that they placed him a room that they knew whenever his system automatically linked with their server, they'd basically be able to trace his files. They may not have been able to open them immediately, but they'd be able to spot them on a system."

"Yet Harpington wanted your brother to add to FrogKiss and set up a surveillance system to watch the employees online, right?"

"Exactly. Hunter had to have known. He's not stupid. He may not have known that his files were being tagged by a special IP address, but he was smart enough to have a separate location to work from. Granted, although he didn't get to do more than hook up his computer to work from, he had a plan."

"What was his plan?"

"To expose Harpington."

"How do we do that?"

We. I leaned across the table and softly kissed her. "There isn't always a happy ending for whistleblowers, so perhaps *you* don't do anything and instead we let my brother."

Her black ponytail swung behind her. "Hunter? Or do you have another brother?"

"No, only one. Hunter."

She reached for my hand. "How can Hunter help us now?"

I held up the MUM stick. "We load all his files, including the online surveillance system he installed at the bequest of Harpington, and send it to the Justice Department."

"Just like that?" She reached for the whiskey and poured herself another glass.

"I know, Jane Bond, it's not sexy, but let the Justice Department wade through figuring out Harpington's intent, knowledge, and dirty proceeds. Let them figure out who he was working with and why. Harpington's already taken enough. Why let him steal any more?"

Her lips touched mine, and I knew she understood.

"I'm sure they have a messenger service at the Newport Heights."

"This late?"

"I want it set up to be hand-delivered to the City of

Huntington Beach, and another copy sent to the Justice Department in Sacramento."

"Oh-kay, what can I do."

"If you happened to have a thumb drive anywhere, that would be great."

She jumped from her chair and onto the king-size bed, where she rummaged through things strewn on the bed. As she went through each item, she tossed it into her backpack. "I thought I had…." When everything was in the bag, she tapped her chin. "Oh, the inside pocket!" She reached into her backpack and withdrew a thumb drive. "It may smell like baby powder, but it works. It's my emergency thumb drive. I always have one with me—somewhere."

She plugged it into the side of my brother's laptop while I called the front desk.

"Hello, Mr. Hughes again."

"How can I help you this morning, Mr. Hughes?"

I glanced at the digital clock on my brother's laptop. 4:10 a.m.

"Yes, it is morning, isn't it?"

"How was your porterhouse and whiskey?"

"Excellent, excellent."

"Would you like to place a breakfast order?"

"No, thank you though. Perhaps later. I'd like to have a courier that the hotel trusts to hand-deliver one document, and then I'd like an overnight package with tracking for another shipment."

"Will this be billed to your room?"

I shook my head. "No, excellent question. I'd like to pay

for these personally with cash."

"Yes, sir. Will the packages be ready within the hour?"

I covered the receiver with my hand and glanced at Carmen. "Can we have the packages ready within the hour?"

"Yes. I can load both the MUM stick and the thumb drive with the decrypted files."

"Yes, we can."

"Excellent. I'll be up to gather your items for shipping. Do you have the addresses? Or may I help with that also?"

"No, thanks. We've got all that covered." I'd no sooner hung up the hotel phone when my cell buzzed with an incoming call. "Oh, hold on, that's my folks." I opened the balcony's sliding door and let the breeze flow into the suite. "Hey, Mom. It's awfully early for you."

"I couldn't sleep. Hank, I thought you were coming home today? Or yesterday."

"I texted Dad, but he probably didn't check his phone. I…." I glanced at Carmen, who smiled. I pointed toward the balcony and stepped outside. "Mom, I'm sorry. There was someone I met and I…." *Didn't want to leave her. How do you leave the woman you're falling for?*

"Hank, is everything okay?"

I shook my head. *No, Mom, it's not. I'm falling head over heels for this woman and it's complicated.* Instead I said what she needed to hear. "Mom, everything's fine. Did you and Dad get home okay?"

"Yes. The flight was fine and your brother…."

"Mom, I'm so sorry."

All I heard was her wounded cries.

"Oh, Mom, don't cry."

"Hank, are you coming home?"

"Home?" I exhaled and brushed my hand through my hair. "Mom…."

Her hand was on my back and her voice a whisper behind me. "Go home, Hank. I'll be okay. Your family needs you."

If I turned and looked at her, I'd never leave. "Yah, Mom." I cleared my throat. "I'll wrap things up here and—"

"Today." Carmen's voice broke the darkness. "She's your mom. Don't make her wait."

I swallowed and nodded. "I'll fly home later today."

"Oh, Hank, that's wonderful. Your dad can meet you at the airport in Eugene."

"I'll text him my flight details when I have them."

"Hank."

"Yah, Mom."

"Please, be careful." Her voice was a plea.

I had long outgrown the dangers of childhood, but now my baby brother had choked to death, my safety was foremost on my mom's mind.

"Always, Mom. Hey, don't worry," I said when I knew it was wishful thinking. She'd always worry. "Love you, Mom."

"Sweetheart, I love you too, and I can't wait to have you back home in Newport."

"Yah, I'll see you later." Our call ended, and I stared at the ocean where Carmen and I had surfed. Everything seemed to be changing. Carmen stood quietly behind me with her arms wrapped around my waist. We'd figured out what Harpington was up to, I'd not only told Carmen how I felt, I showed her, and Hunter's final work was complete. I had everything. Yet it felt like my happiness was flashing by me and I couldn't slow the speed.

CHAPTER **THIRTY-FIVE**

The MUM stick was in an overnight envelope and on its way to the Justice Department in Sacramento, and a thumb drive would be hand-delivered to the City of Huntington Beach. At the last minute, we decided that the set of Hunter's spreadsheets should be sent to the one place who would do the most with it—the LA Times. An e-mail with links to his other files was sent to the Orange County LA Times bureau editor from Hunter's e-mail.

I knelt on the bed beside Hank. "I never knew how empty my heart was until I met you." My hands held his masculine, jagged face. "You've given me something I'll cherish forever."

His hazel eyes swirled in color. "What? What did I give you?"

"Forgiveness. Compassion. Honesty. When you walked into your brother's hospital room, your kindness allowed me to forgive myself for not saving Hunter. You gave me that. Your feelings for me changed me." Tears streamed down my face. "It'll never be goodbye between us." My lips trembled when I kissed him. "Me gustas."

I took off his T-shirt that I had borrowed and dropped it to the floor beside the bed. He reached behind his head and pulled off his shirt. He slid out of his trunks, and we lay beside each other where our bodies met—flesh against flesh. There wasn't any ocean between us. There was no space, only our love as he moved inside me, his hand on my back pressing us closer together. Neither of us spoke. Our feelings for each other bridged the hurt I saw in his eyes and felt in his touch. *Please don't leave.* I silenced my heart's desire for what I knew Hank needed—Oregon, family, stability. I could give him love and a big family, but California wasn't home.

Tears streamed down my face, and Hank's eyes brimmed. "Carmen, I adore you."

I nodded and pressed my forehead against his. "Me gustas." It felt like I was breaking in two. But for this sliver of morning, this strong, beautiful man was mine. I stared into his eyes and felt how much he cared for me as he moved in and out of me with a deep desire to please me. He always thought of me first.

How do I let go? My heart only knew that what I wanted wasn't as important as my gentle giant. Hank placed everyone before himself. It was time for someone to put him first. And I would be that person in his life who cared for him enough to let him go. I didn't know how, only that I would. Doing right by him was more important than anything in my life.

His lips brushed my neck, and my hands cradled his head as I inhaled his scent, feeling his flesh against mine, imprinting him on me. *I will wait for you forever.*

CHAPTER THIRTY-SIX

My abuelita placed the newspaper beside my morning coffee and vitamins. She was forever leaving vitamins for me, as if enough calcium and iron would mend a broken heart. Hank and I spoke every day, but the distance was greater than either of us had imagined. Four weeks without seeing him, and I was beginning to think maybe it was just a summer fling. I tossed the vitamins in my mouth and washed them down with strong, black chicory coffee.

"Mija, what did you think about the story on the front page?"

The food section was in front of me. "Plums, pears, and how to perfect jam."

I shrugged. "Sure, I could learn how to jam. Why not? It's not like I have an active social life now or anytime soon."

"Jam?" she called from the pantry. "Well, yes it is quite a jam, but I thought maybe this would bring you greater happiness."

"*Jam?* You thought jam would bring me happiness. Sure, why not. I may as well get my first cat and make it official." I leaned my head on the kitchen table and stared at the folded newspaper. The edge of the front section stuck out, and it looked like Mr. Harpington was staring at me. *What?* I lifted my head and grabbed the paper.

"Ay Dios mio."

A photo of Michael Harpington was on the front page. The photo wasn't very flattering, and the headline was worse.

Hotel Founder and Owner Charged with Money Laundering

Huntington Beach: The founder and owner of The Point Resort has been charged with larceny, money laundering, and breaches of the Cybercrimes Act.

Michael Harpington was charged on Wednesday and posted a million-dollar bail, and is to appear in court on August 13.

Investigators reported that during the period of October 2015 to July this year, Harpington defrauded the hotel of $1.5 million and laundered in excess of billions. It is reported that as CEO and founder, Harpington manipulated the system and converted the money to his own use.

While surveillance of employees in the workplace is often frowned upon in the hotel industry, the hidden cameras in the staff changing rooms, where they have a reasonable expectation of privacy, prompted further investigation into Harpington's cyber activity. Harpington was charged with acts of cybercrime for unauthorized surveillance of employees in the workplace and their online activity that extended to their personal banking and financial data.

The US Justice Department reports that money laundering isn't a new trend affecting hotels, however it has stepped up its focus on resort properties.

"Oh, damn!" I held the paper and stared at the print. It had been weeks since Hank and I sent the anonymous packages to the Justice Department, City of Huntington Beach, and the LA Times. But it worked.

"I didn't even know he was arrested," I said in the direction of the pantry. "Once my weeklong suspension ended, I've kept to my own business. I haven't even looked in Mr. Harpington's direction."

"Good for you, mija. He will get what he deserves."

"Well, he deserves to gag on a hidden camera and be strangled with the wires."

The screen door to the patio opened and Papà walked into the kitchen with a bag of oranges and a brown paper bag.

"Buenos días, hija." He kissed my forehead.

"Good morning, *Padre*." He placed the oranges on the chair beside me and the bag in front of me. "Qué pasa?"

"I read the paper." He tilted his chin with pride, and I knew where my stubbornness came from.

"Did you?" I smiled. "I read it too. So, what's with the bag?"

He shrugged. "I guess you won't know unless you open

it."

"Is it going to explode?"

He fanned his hand at me. "Carmen, such nonsense."

I opened the bag and pulled out a bottle of nasal spray. An index card was taped to it. "Allergy spray" was written in red in my father's penmanship. I placed it on the table and reached in the bag. A white envelope with his penmanship in blue marker read, "Gas Money." I opened the envelope, and it was filled with hundreds.

"Ay Dios mio."

He nodded toward the bag. "There's more."

I dumped the contents on the table. Two canisters of Pringles, a bag of M&M's, box of Junior Mints, big pack of Little Debbie's Nutty Bars, and a larger pack of Little Debbie's Swiss Cake Rolls were strapped together with electrical tape. The index card was written in green: "Travelin' Vittles."

"Travelin' vittles. Allergy spray. Gas money." I looked up. "Are we going on a trip?"

He slowly shook his head and folded his hands together. "No, but I think you may." He reached into his pants pocket, withdrew a key ring, and placed it on the table between us. "Since you wouldn't take any of your mamá's money for school, it's been collecting interest in your account. I used that interest to buy you something a little more reliable to get you to Oregon."

"Oregon?" My lip trembled and my eyes filled with tears. "Papà."

"Carmen, whatever you do, choose with your heart."

"I'm falling in love—with Hank."

"And I'm sure, mija, he's already head over heels in love with you," he said.

"Papà, I miss him so much it hurts."

He smiled with his eyes. "I know, mija."

I jumped from my seat and wrapped my arms around him. His spicy cologne was the scent of my childhood. "Te amo, Papá."

"Te amo, Carmen. Voy a extrañarete, mi hija."

"I'll miss you too, *Papá*."

He reached around me and patted my backside. "Go, look at your car."

I squealed. "I can't believe you got me a car."

"Don't get excited until you see it." Abuelita laughed, then she kissed the top of her son's head. "That was very kind of you, hijo."

"You're not the only one who gets to spoil my only child."

She chuckled.

I ran outside with them on my heels.

"It's used, but it's easy on your wallet and the environment, and from what I read those Oregonians are pretty serious about being green."

I stared at the compact-sized hybrid that was a bright, neon green, and laughed. "Oh, wow, *Papá*."

The shiny shade of green was something any Oregon Duck fan would not only notice, but appreciate with equal measure. I turned and hugged him. "Papà, it's perfect. I love it. Thank you."

My last two weeks at the Waterfront were filled with many goodbyes and well wishes.

"So, I don't suppose you know anything about the files that put the final nail in Harpington's coffin, do you?" Bogart stood beside his wife.

I shrugged. "No clue."

Katie shook her head. "You're a terrible liar."

"The LA Times published parts of the financial documents that show the extent of Harpington's involvement. The files were sent to them anonymously," Bogart said.

"I guess whoever sent it to them didn't want to be identified."

"Or credited with uncovering the hidden surveillance," Katie said. "That's huge."

"Enough talk about Harpington. I want to remember how we were together at the beginning when the hotel opened its doors. We started our jobs here when the hotel was new, and hung on during tough times. I'll never forget you guys."

They smiled. "We'll never forget you or what you did."

I held up my hand and grinned. "Sure, I may have the technical background and more than enough incentive to do exactly what the anonymous whistleblower did, but have you ever known me to be modest?"

They nodded. "Yes, you're very modest."

I shook my head. "Nah. I'd blow my own horn if I'd blown the whistle on the hotel, and I'd severely sprain my hand from patting myself on the back for a job well done." I grimaced. "No, if it were me, you and everyone else would know all about it, because I would never shut up. So, while I'd love to take credit for it, I can't. All I do is take the guests' cars and park them. You know I'm no vigilante. I'm just a valet."

CHAPTER **THIRTY-SEVEN**

"So… if I were in Oregon tonight, what would we do?"

Carmen's voice in my ear shut the world out. She was the salve for happiness.

"Oh, well, let's see." I leaned against my car. "Well, would you be in Portland or here in Newport."

"Newport. Where you live."

I nodded. "Okay. Well, since I'm off work and it's the start of the weekend, I'd take you to dinner."

"Where?"

"Oh, you want details."

"Si."

"Depends on what you're in the mood for."

"Nuh-uh. If you had to arrange the entire night, what would we do?"

"Carmen, if you were in Newport with me, I'd take you to my temporary apartment, which is above my parents' garage, by the way—" I laughed. "—I'd lock the door, and I wouldn't ever let you leave."

I closed my eyes and listened to her laughter. I swore the scent of coconuts wafted in the air. I opened my eyes and a sporty little neon-green car turned onto our street.

"So, no dinner then?" she said.

The car slowed and seemed to be looking for a house. "Girl, you'll never go hungry when you're with me."

She giggled. "Good, because I've got a hunger only you can satisfy."

"I miss you," I said, eyeing the green little coupe.

"Oh, Hank, I've missed you more than you know."

"Not possible. I'm in love with you." It flew out of my mouth before I could retrieve it to the safety of my heart.

For a moment there wasn't any response, and the green car stopped in the middle of the street.

"Hank, I'm so glad you said that, because I love you, too. I'm madly, head over heels in love with you. *Te amo, te amo, te amo.*"

My chest swelled. "Oh, Carmen. You've just made me the happiest man—ever." I laughed.

"What's so funny?"

"My luck. We finally utter those three little words to each other and it's over the phone." I ran my hand across my head when the car stopped in front of my parents' house. I glanced in the passenger side window but boxes blocked the view of the driver. "Babe, hold up. I'm sorry, but some car's here that I don't recognize."

The driver side door opened, and I lost my breath.

"Hola."

"You're here."

"I'm here."

She walked toward me in a yellow sundress and white sandals. I stared at her and then the car. "Normally, the princess kisses the little green frog instead of driving one to my castle." I smiled. "I really like your car."

"Gracias." Her hair fell around her shoulders and bounced with every step.

"You're beautiful."

"I'm unemployed."

"So, you left your job and came right to me."

"Isn't that the breaks," she said with a smile.

"Yes, and as a rule I wouldn't have it any other way."

THE **END**

ACKNOWLEDGEMENTS

I had to learn two languages when writing Rule Breakers: Spanish and computer code.

My limited Español was broadened and enriched by my beautiful niece, Laura Juliette Billiter. "Carmen" was modeled after LJ, who shared her love of the "hot Latino guys on the telenovelas," her terms of endearment for her mamá and papá, and her heart. Anytime I texted LJ with a question, she'd respond immediately and follow it up with, "Happy to help." If more people were like my twenty-something-year-old niece the world would be an even better place. So this book was always written for you LJ. Love you.

To LJ's father, my big brother, Stephen Thaddeus Billiter or Tbone. I pester you on a pretty consistent basis and you never get frustrated with me—or at least you don't show it! Thank you. Since childhood—when you taught me how to spell your name: Step-hen—to forty-something years later, when you created the fictitious MUM stick and its acronym, my work is smarter and better because of your generous spirit. Thank you, brother. Xoxo

To my Geek Squad: Tighe Fagan, who patiently answered each and every question I had pertaining to computers, codes, and programming. Thank you for geeking it down for me and then allowing yourself to be a professor in my book. When I asked your permission for your name to be attached to this professor, your texted replay was gold: "Bucket list: be a character in a romance novel—check." I don't think it's the end of Professor Fagan….

And to Matt Roberts, my web designer extraordinaire, who also helped brainstorm the plot for Rule Breakers. Keep watching computer-nerd movies! Thank you for always answering my long-worded texts.

To my grief support: I also had to approach a topic where research can be tricky. Grief is not something people are often excited to discuss, but I found a real gem with licensed therapist Debra Cochren, who shared her insight into grief. Thank you for trusting me with your stories and experience.

To my publisher & book family: Becky Johnson and Hot Tree Publishing—Meeting you and everyone from Hot Tree in Atlanta at the RT Booklovers Convention, was a once in a lifetime moment! The immediate connection I had with other Hot Tree authors made sense because you're at the helm. Becky, you've created a niche in the industry because your authors are as valued and supported as the work itself. It's a remarkable combination that inspires me toward my best. Thank you for allowing me and my work to be included in the brilliance of Hot Tree Publishing.

Liv Ventura—Since meeting you, now when I read my edits they're in an Australian accent! Thank you for unearthing my best and then recognizing when I do! That's pretty awesome. And now for a hotel elevator that talks to its guests. It's up next and I think he'll have an Aussie accent.

To my husband, Ron, & family:

Ron, the door to our bedroom is closed often when I'm writing. Thank you for understanding and supporting my passion to write. And for being the toughest editor I've ever had the privilege of learning from. You are my muse. When you're around, happily ever after isn't too far behind. We are #bettertogether

To my children—Dylan, Max, Austin, Kyle, and especially my two little ones at home—Ciara and Super Cooper—thank you. You make me laugh at the small stuff and it's all small stuff.

To my siblings—Suzanne Billiter Cragin, Stephen Billiter & Patrick Billiter—I know at least three books will be purchased on release day. Thank you. Your encouragement and belief in me means more than you will ever know. We are #BilliterStrong.

And to my readers—what a journey. From reading my weekly newspaper column to my published romances, thank you for following me and my work. I am always humbled by your support and good wishes. Thank you!

ABOUT THE **AUTHOR**

Mary Billiter is a weekly newspaper columnist and fiction author. She also has novels published under the pen name, "Pumpkin Spice."

Mary resides in the Cowboy State with her unabashedly bald husband, their combined children, and runaway dog. She does her best writing (in her head) on her daily runs in wild, romantic, beautiful Wyoming.

CONNECT WITH MARY:
WWW.MARYBILLITER.COM/
WWW.TWITTER.COM/MARYBILLITER
WWW.FACEBOOK.COM/MARYMBILLITER

ABOUT THE **PUBLISHER**

Hot Tree Publishing opened its doors in 2015 with an aspiration to bring quality fiction to the world of readers. With the initial focus on romance and a wide spread of romance sub-genres, we envision opening up to alternative genres in the near future.

Firmly seated in the industry as a leading editing provider to independent authors and small publishing houses, Hot Tree Publishing is the sister company to Hot Tree Editing, founded in 2012. Having established in-house editing and promotions, plus having a well-respected market presence, Hot Tree Publishing endeavors to be a leader in bringing quality stories to the world of readers.

Interested in discovering more amazing reads brought to you by Hot Tree Publishing or perhaps you're interested in submitting a manuscript and joining the HTPubs family? Either way, head over to the website for information:

WWW.HOTTREEPUBLISHING.COM